W9-CIJ-535

"We're supposed to be easy with each other," Keir said.

"We're supposed to have been lovers," he continued.

Darcy gulped. "Um—yes."

"So some practicing wouldn't go amiss."

"Um—no," she acknowledged.

Changing back into her character, she pushed at him, they struggled, and he gave her a punishing kiss.

Darcy parted her lips. Then it became a real kiss. A deep kiss.

When it ended, Keir drew back to frown. Was he going to ask what she had been doing and accuse her of breaking the rules?

"Enough passion?" she inquired.

ELIZABETH OLDFIELD's writing career started as a teenage hobby, when she had articles published. However, on her marriage the creative instinct was diverted into the production of a daughter and son. A decade later, when her husband's job took them to Singapore, she resumed writing and had her first romance novel accepted in 1982. Now hooked on the genre, she produces an average of three books a year. They live in London, England, and Elizabeth travels widely to authenticate the background of her books.

Books by Elizabeth Oldfield

HARLEQUIN PRESENTS
1636—DESIGNED TO ANNOY
1676—SUDDEN FIRE
1773—LOVE'S PRISONER
1800—DARK VICTORY

Don't miss any of our special offers. Write to us at the following address for information on our newest releases.

Harlequin Reader Service
U.S.: 3010 Walden Ave., P.O. Box 1325, Buffalo, NY 14269
Canadian: P.O. Box 609, Fort Erie, Ont. L2A 5X3

ELIZABETH OLDFIELD

Fast and Loose

Harlequin Books

TORONTO • NEW YORK • LONDON
AMSTERDAM • PARIS • SYDNEY • HAMBURG
STOCKHOLM • ATHENS • TOKYO • MILAN
MADRID • WARSAW • BUDAPEST • AUCKLAND

If you purchased this book without a cover you should be aware
that this book is stolen property. It was reported as "unsold and
destroyed" to the publisher, and neither the author nor the
publisher has received any payment for this "stripped book."

ISBN 0-373-11831-7

FAST AND LOOSE

First North American Publication 1996.

Copyright © 1996 by Elizabeth Oldfield.

All rights reserved. Except for use in any review, the reproduction or
utilization of this work in whole or in part in any form by any electronic,
mechanical or other means, now known or hereafter invented, including
xerography, photocopying and recording, or in any information storage
or retrieval system, is forbidden without the written permission of the
publisher, Harlequin Enterprises Limited, 225 Duncan Mill Road,
Don Mills, Ontario, Canada M3B 3K9.

All characters in this book have no existence outside the imagination of
the author and have no relation whatsoever to anyone bearing the same
name or names. They are not even distantly inspired by any individual
known or unknown to the author, and all incidents are pure invention.

This edition published by arrangement with Harlequin Books S.A.

® and TM are trademarks of the publisher. Trademarks indicated with
® are registered in the United States Patent and Trademark Office, the
Canadian Trade Marks Office and in other countries.

Printed in U.S.A.

CHAPTER ONE

DARCY frowned at the young man who sat on the other side of the low mahogany table. 'I was stood in the lobby waiting for you for almost half an hour,' she told him.

'Sorry. Had trouble finding a taxi,' Maurice Cantwell declared, fingering the apricot and white spotted bowtie which he wore with a pale apricot sharkskin suit. 'Though you could've waited in here.'

'But if I'd sat immobile where people can take their time and look someone might've recognised me,' she protested.

'So? Other actresses like to be recognised. Other actresses...' His words dried as he looked beyond her to the entrance of the oak-panelled bar. 'Hi, there!' he called, waving an eager hand. 'We're over here.'

As her agent put down his cocktail and leapt to his feet in readiness to greet someone whom he had clearly expected Darcy's lips compressed. She had thought his invitation to dinner at the Brierly Hotel was odd, but—dumbo!—she ought to have guessed that it might not necessarily be just the two of them.

Maurice had his fingers thrust into endless pies, and now it seemed that he might be attempting to swing one of the deals which he habitually indulged in and that she had been asked along as feminine decoration and some form of inducement. While the refined and dignified Brierly had been chosen as the venue in order to impress.

Darcy gritted her teeth. Sitting with her back to the door, she was unable to see who was approaching, but she refused to spend the evening making small talk with some impresario for Maurice's benefit. She refused to be exploited.

Her agent took a step past her to welcome the new arrival. 'Great to have a chance to meet you at last,' he said in what, for him, were surprisingly sincere, reverential tones. 'I'm a big admirer of both your acting and directing skills, though it's a long time now since you've acted.'

'As I get older I find I prefer to tell others what to do, rather than be told myself,' replied a man in a smoky American drawl laced with an ironic inflexion.

Darcy froze. She was sure—almost—that she recognised the voice. Whipping her head round, she looked up. Her green eyes flew wide open. Her jaw dropped. Her mind seemed to implode. Towering above her was a tall figure—a broad-shouldered, narrow-hipped and utterly virile figure. The expected dinner guest was a man whom she had last seen seven years ago and whom she had never wanted to see again—Keir Robards!

She gawked at him. Like her agent's dress style, his was also different from that of the hotel's other, conservatively suited male customers, but whereas Maurice had gone for overkill he had opted for understatement. He wore cowboy boots, faded denims and an ancient black blazer thrown over a dark blue poplin shirt. His appearance was casual yet somehow he contrived to look smarter than every other man in the bar.

'You two know each other,' Maurice announced, with the gleeful air of a television host who—surprise, surprise—was bringing together a pair of old, dear, but long-lost friends.

Realising that she was still gawking, Darcy closed her mouth. She wanted to murder Maurice.

'We did,' she said, tautly placing their relationship in the past—where she intended it to remain.

'Good evening, Darcy,' Keir Robards said, and held down a large, tanned hand.

His handclasp came accompanied by a smile—a slow, crooked smile which, once upon a time, would have had her crumbling into a pathetically adoring heap. But no longer. Darcy nodded, withdrew her hand, sat back and crossed long, black-stockinged legs. Seven years on she was made of sterner stuff.

Nevertheless, the pressure of his fingers and the feel of his skin against hers had had an annoyingly sensitising effect. It made her aware of the way some physical contact, however mundane, could start the adrenalin spurting. It had also created a tension.

'What are you doing here?' she enquired, attempting to appear nonchalant and unconcerned but hearing herself sound dyspeptic.

Although Keir Robards had been consigned to history and she had not thought about him for... oh, ages, as she had waited in the lobby memories had relentlessly surfaced—of the last time she had visited the hotel, which had been the time of their final encounter, when she had made a monumental *fool* of herself.

Then, with her cheeks a feverish raspberry and her nerves twanging like crazed harp strings, she had dashed from his bedroom, hurled herself between the closing doors of a most obligingly placed lift and, on reaching ground level, had galloped across the lobby and out into the night.

Darcy sipped from her glass of sparkling water. The memory still made her squirm. And now, after intruding so discomfitingly into her consciousness earlier, for Keir Robards to appear in person was a bizarre coincidence—one which tempted her to make another hasty exit. But was *he* involved in a deal with Maurice? His elegant calm made a stark contrast to her agent's ponytailed flamboyance, yet she supposed it was possible.

'I'm staying at the hotel. I've been in London on business,' he told her, 'just for a couple of days. I fly back to the States tomorrow.'

'Busy guy,' Maurice murmured approvingly. 'Sit down, sit down. Take my seat,' he insisted when Keir looked around to draw up a chair. 'You must have a drink,' he said, and, after establishing his guest's preference, he rapidly organised a gin and tonic. 'I was on the point of telling Darcy about the new situation.'

Keir shot her a look. 'You don't know?'

'Know what?' Darcy asked in bewilderment. She frowned up at Maurice. 'Would you kindly tell me what it is you're talking about?'

'The play,' he said.

In a month's time she was due to fly to the States to start rehearsing the female lead in a new, hard-hitting emotional drama which, after two weeks of previews in Washington, would première with much fanfare on Broadway. Darcy felt a trickle of alarm. She had thought everything was cut and dried, but there had, it seemed, been changes. Yet how could this have anything to do with Keir Robards?

'There's bad news—and good news,' Maurice went on.

'What's the bad news?' she enquired, thinking that it was always better to confront that first.

'Bill Shapiro's been forced to withdraw.'

'Oh, no!' Darcy exclaimed in dismay. 'Why?'

'He's had a quadruple heart bypass which means he'll be out of the scene for three months min. Poor Bill,' the young man said, more automatically than sympathetically. 'But the good news is...' he paused to beam down at the American '...Keir's come to the rescue.'

Darcy's tension tightened as if turned by a ratchet. Her heart kicked behind her ribs. 'You've—you've taken over as director?' she faltered, struggling desperately up from the cocooning depths of her maroon velvet armchair.

Keir nodded. 'I have.'

She perched, ramrod-stiff, on the edge of the chair. 'But——' she started to bleat.

'I knew you'd be thrilled,' Maurice declared, and gave a loud guffaw of satisfaction which boomeranged around the bar. In a lesser establishment it would have raised eyebrows and swivelled heads but the Brierly's clientele were too well-bred to react.

'"Thrilled" appears to be something of an exaggeration,' Keir murmured, watching her, then looked up as a bell-boy in a grey brass-buttoned uniform appeared between the tables, holding aloft a board on which was written 'Telephone for Mr Robards'. 'Excuse me,' he said, rising, and, with a word to the youth, he strode out to take his call at one of the telephones that were discreetly sited on the far side of the lobby.

'We were both happy with Bill Shapiro directing,' Maurice said hastily. 'Though, let's face it, as the play is your dream ticket to stardom we'd have been happy to go along with most any director unless he was a real doggo. Robards isn't a doggo; he's the *crème de la crème*.'

Darcy frowned down into the cut-crystal tumbler of sparkling mineral water which she suddenly realised she was holding in her fingers. Holding tight. Very tight. Stardom did not bother her—what mattered was her wonderfully challenging role. The observation that there were few meaty parts for actresses might have been a cliché, yet, as clichés often did, it contained much truth, and she had been savouring the prospect of getting to grips. But now...

'I don't want to work with him,' she said.

Maurice affected a look of frog-eyed surprise. 'Why ever not?'

Darcy had two reasons. Valid reasons. What she had come to think of as the bedroom incident was the first, though no one knew about that—praise be—but the second reason, and by far the more important, lived in the public domain—at least a part of it did. A line cut between her brows. However, the real source of her hostility, the crucial, damning factor, remained a secret, locked away at the back of her mind. It was a secret which, after much agonising, she had learned to live with.

Darcy sat back. 'You know why not,' she said impatiently.

'You can't be bothered about that episode between Robards and Rupert all those years ago?' the young man protested as though—gee whizz!—the thought had only just occurred to him. He dropped down into the empty chair. 'Come on, kiddo, artistic differences happen. They're an occupational hazard and nothing to get uptight about.'

Her chin lifted. 'My father feeling forced to withdraw from a production for the first and only time in an illustrious forty-year career just *happened*?' Darcy enquired, a glacial edge to her voice. 'Keir Robards was an innocent bystander?'

'Look, Rupert was in his sixties, and taking instruction from a guy of under thirty who at that point had only directed on a couple of occasions could've seemed infra dig and been a bit of a strain. It's understandable. Human nature.'

She glared. 'Which is supposed to mean that it was my father who was at fault?' she demanded.

Maurice sighed. While some pride and filial support was to be applauded, in his opinion Darcy took the role of devoted daughter far too seriously. She also possessed a faulty perspective.

OK, Sir Rupert Weston had been an endearing old codger and an upper-echelon actor, but it was a well-known fact that the guy had been no saint. Anything but. And yet, he philosophised, it was also human nature for kids to dote uncritically on their fathers.

'All it means is that you and Robards are a very different combination from him and your pa,' Maurice replied, as if soothing a foot-stamping and sadly misguided three-year-old. He stood up. 'Everything OK?' he asked, smiling at his guest, who had returned.

Keir nodded. 'And with you?' he enquired, his eyes flicking down to where Darcy sat solemn-faced.

'Wonderful,' Maurice claimed. 'There's no doubt Darcy would've zapped the critics under Bill Shapiro's direction——' she received a flattering smile '—but with you calling the shots she's destined to take the Big Apple by storm. You're sharp, energetic, imaginative.' Now it was Keir's turn to be shone a flattering smile. 'A guy with a firm concept of what he wants and who isn't afraid to go for it.'

Keir lifted a brow. 'You reckon?'

'And how,' Maurice enthused, deaf to the pithiness of the comment. 'Didn't have a chance to break the news to her before because this has been one hectic week,' he continued. 'On Monday a client who's always causing me pain——'

As her agent rattled off into a non-stop and unstoppable account of his week's trials and tribulations Darcy sneaked a look at the man who had sat down opposite her again. Despite the intervening years, he was much as she remembered him. The odd strand of silver now gleamed amid the thick, straight dark blond hair which brushed his collar, and the vertical creases on either side of his mouth were etched deeper, but his eyes remained a clear cobalt-blue beneath brows which were uncompromisingly straight. His jawline was still granite-cut and his nose aquiline.

As an actor Keir Robards had collected female fans with insolent ease and yet, while she, too, had considered him a sight to make any girl's knees turn to water, his good looks had not been the appeal. What she had found magnetic was his intelligence, his style and a sense of inner steel which had made him seem ... dangerous. Darcy felt a sharp pang of distress. He *had* been dangerous, as she knew to her cost.

That steely quality remained and with the years had come a sureness. The younger Keir Robards had been quietly confident but the mature Keir Robards was a man of authority, a man of stature, a man with whom one did not mess.

As she gazed at him from beneath her lashes two emotions travelled through her—emotions which contradicted each other yet were intertwined. She felt a strong hostility—and an equally strong attraction. A shadow crossed her face. How could that be? It made no sense. She loathed and despised Keir Robards. End of story.

Finishing his recital, Maurice grabbed his glass from the table and drained it in one gulp. 'I must be off,' he declared.

Darcy's head snapped up and she looked at him in astonishment. 'Off?' she repeated. 'You mean you're not having dinner?'

'Nah. You don't need me around. Much better if I vamoose and leave you two beautiful people to talk things over together in a cosy tête-à-tête. Don't you agree, Keir?'

His guest had been watching their interplay and he gave a dry smile. 'That's what you arranged.'

'Besides,' Maurice went on, when Darcy started to protest, 'I have another appointment fixed for this evening.'

As he beckoned to the waiter and paid for the drinks Darcy's green eyes began to burn. She had been set up! Guessing she would not wish even to meet Keir Robards, let alone work with him, Maurice had prepared a trap.

Firstly, he had delayed advising her of the change in director, which he had apparently known about for days. Secondly, he had contacted the American and fixed for him to have dinner with her. Thirdly, this evening he had been late—on purpose, she thought angrily—which meant that he must have chickened out of dropping his bombshell when they were alone and when she could have properly voiced her dissent. When she could have laid it on the line that she was—as in *definitely*, no ifs nor buts, come hell or high water—pulling out of the play.

And now his intentions were clear; he expected her to be beguiled by the magnetic Mr Robards and swap her dissent for slavering acquiescence. A thought occurred. Had Maurice known how besotted she had been seven years ago? No. She had not started acting in earnest and been his client then. But he would be alert to Keir's heartthrob status so it made no difference.

'I'm sure you can cancel your appointment,' Darcy said, shooting her agent a fierce, slit-eyed look which warned him that she had realised the game he was playing and was unamused.

He shook his head, pony-tail swinging. ''Fraid not.'

'But Maurice——' she began, switching from ferocity to a somewhat frantic appeal.

'I understand the food is excellent here and I've arranged to foot the bill, so enjoy,' he instructed, and after bestowing 'mwah-mwah' kisses to both her cheeks the young man made his farewells and hurried away.

'Louse,' she muttered.

'Are you referring to Maurice or to me?' Keir enquired from across the table.

She looked at him. She had not realised that she had spoken out loud. 'Maurice,' she said, though thinking that he qualified for the description too. 'He's not to be trusted. He's always been a tricksy individual and he always will be.'

'Then why keep him on as your agent?'

Darcy had wondered about that herself. She had also mulled over the irony of someone who was not very good at show business and certainly not as ambitious as one was meant to be being represented by a pushy wheeler-dealer like Maurice.

'Because he has an impeccable instinct for identifying good parts,' she replied, which was true—most of the time.

Keir's blue eyes held hers in a level look. 'You also keep him on because his father used to be your father's agent.'

Darcy stiffened. She did not want to talk about her father—not with him. No, thank you. It was a no-go area, sacred ground where Keir, as the infidel, had no right to trespass. Where he was banned. But hadn't his comment been a condemnation?

'So I'm carrying on a family tradition. There's nothing wrong with that,' she said defensively.

'But there is something wrong with Maurice keeping stumm about Bill Shapiro and not telling you of this evening's arrangements,' he remarked, and lifted his glass to his lips.

As he sampled his gin and tonic his eyes took a journey over her. Starting at the top of her burnished sable-brown head, they toured her face—the high cheekbones, almond-shaped green eyes, full, crushed-strawberry mouth—fell to linger for a moment on the pout of her breasts, swept lower over her body to her hips and went down the length of her legs until the low table masked any further view.

He lifted his gaze. 'You've grown up,' he said.

Darcy bridled. His look had been a leisurely and de-tailed inspection. She felt as if he had removed every stitch of her clothing, piece by lazily tossed-aside piece, and surveyed her naked. Stark naked.

'People do,' she retorted. 'I was eighteen when we last met, whereas now I'm——'

'A sophisticated twenty-five,' he said.

Because Maurice had told her on the telephone to 'dress in your best' Darcy was wearing a slim-skirted black linen suit with a spaghetti-strapped coffee-coloured lace camisole. She had also made up her face with un-usual care—bronze eyeshadow, sooty mascara, the works—and had shampooed her hair which swung in silky sable-brown curls around her shoulders.

She knew she was looking good and, although she told herself that she did not give a fig about whatever Keir Robards might say, it was impossible to prevent a glow of feminine pleasure.

'Thanks,' she said curtly.

Keir's eyes fell again. 'Who still has the most tempting curves,' he added.

Sophisticated or not, Darcy flushed scarlet. His comment held a wealth of meaning, for when she had visited his room at the Brierly all those years ago the dress she had worn had been daringly low-cut and, as she had hoped and intended, Keir had been fascinated by the honeyed swell of her breasts.

Darcy fought an urge to yank her jacket across her chest and fasten each and every button. All of a sudden her camisole seemed woefully revealing, and from the continued dip of his gaze he appeared to be fascinated by her lace-covered bosom now.

'Couldn't the play be postponed until Mr Shapiro is well again?' she enquired, in a determined and rather desperate switch of subject.

Calmly raising his eyes to hers, Keir shook his head. 'It'd mean too much upheaval for too many people, you must realise that. And if the theatre slots went it might take a year before they could be replaced.' He dragged a hand through the spikes of tawny hair which persisted in falling across his brow, raking them back. 'You haven't worked with either Bill Shapiro before or with me, so what makes you prefer him?'

She shot him a startled look. Didn't he know? He had to. He must. It was neon-lit to her. But of course Keir might consider the events of the past to be of little consequence.

While his regarding her piece of lunacy as insignificant would be an enormous relief—perhaps his reference to her curves had been random and the bedroom incident had faded from his mind?—that he could be indifferent to what had happened with her father—*to* her father—made her burn with raw resentment. How callous. How cruel. Yet she supposed it was possible. One person's catastrophe could be another person's hiccup, and everything had happened a long time ago.

Darcy took a sip of sparkling water. His question had sounded rational and reasonable so she would answer in a similar manner; but what did she say?

'I prefer Mr Shapiro,' she began, 'because, well, for a while now I've had it fixed in my head that he'd be directing, and I've become used to the idea. And I liked it. And when we spoke on the phone he seemed a pleasant individual. And...' Aware of waffling, Darcy heard her voice fade away.

'And you've never lusted after him,' Keir completed.

To her fury, she felt her cheeks start to burn again. He had not forgotten what had been the most embarrassing incident in her entire life. Damn it. Damn him. But he need not think that she would be covered in girlish confusion this time.

Darcy had once acted the role of Cleopatra at stage school and now she eyed him with icy and regal disdain. 'I've never lusted after you,' she declared.

A smile played around the corners of his mouth. 'No kidding?'

'I had a crush, that was all. A mild, innocent schoolgirl crush, which lasted for an extremely short time.'

'And your innocence lasted for an extremely short time after that because you became a hot item with the young Lothario Gideon McCall.'

At his mention of the actor whom she had once dated,
Darcy frowned. The distaste in Keir's tone indicated that
he could be recalling how, on the expiry of their romance, Gideon had spoken about it to the Press. Her
frown deepened. If Keir did not approve of Gideon's
lurid and elaborately fabricated kiss-and-tell which had
been pounced on by the tabloid newspapers, neither did
she; though it had served one useful purpose.

'Gideon was a humanoid calamity, but regrettably
when I was younger——' she shone a cheesy smile '—I
did not have such great taste in men.'

'Ouch,' Keir murmured.

'However, now I'm far more discerning.'

He lifted a brow. 'Heaven be praised for maturity. So
why are you reluctant to work with me?' Keir asked,
returning to his earlier enquiry.

Having stalwartly denied her first reason, Darcy was
left with the second. But by the time the so-called 'artistic differences' with her father had occurred she had
been avoiding Keir Robards like the plague so he had
not been aware of her feelings, her conclusions, nor of
the blame which she had later apportioned.

She bit deep into her lip. She balked at revealing any
of this now, balked at reviving hurtful memories which
could, if she threw caution to the winds, lead to the
flinging of a dramatic indictment. What was the point?
Her much loved father was dead. Nothing could be
changed.

'You're afraid that as I've not directed since—
when?—last fall I might be rusty?' he said, when she
remained silent.

As he had hesitated Keir had brushed his fingertips
across his mouth in thought and drawn her gaze. He had
a thin upper lip and a fuller, sensual lower one. Once

she had spent hours fantasising about those lips, that mouth—how it would feel when he kissed her, how after much delirious kissing, when her own mouth was softly bruised and tender, his would move slowly and tantalisingly down her naked body; how his lips would brush across the peaks of her aching nipples, how he would open his mouth and——

Darcy dragged her eyes away. What was she thinking?

'Correct,' she declared, grabbing gratefully, if untruthfully, at his suggestion.

While she never sought out information about Keir Robards it was impossible to avoid the occasional newspaper paragraph or comment made by a colleague within the theatre. So she knew that he would accept a directing assignment—sometimes a stage play, sometimes a film but, during the past seven years, never again in England—then vanish from public view for perhaps several months before he became involved in the next. What he did in between times was a mystery.

'I often have gaps and yet—touch wood——' Keir leaned forward to press long, blunt-tipped fingers to the table '—so far I've managed to do a good job. I intend to do a good job this time.'

And never mind any damage you might inflict on others, Darcy thought bitterly.

Pushing back his cuff, he checked the vintage Rolex watch which was strapped to his broad wrist. 'It's eight-thirty,' he said. 'Why don't we find our table and carry on talking in the restaurant?'

Darcy clenched her fists, the fingernails biting into her palms. She did not want to dine with him. No, no, no. What she wanted to do was deliver a series of ringing slaps to his freshly shaven jaw, spin on her heel and march out; but that would be a big mistake.

Although Keir might direct intermittently, he possessed considerable status, and if she antagonised him too much it could rebound and damage her career. People in the business would notice her withdrawal from the play and ask questions, and all it would need would be a comment from him about Darcy Weston being unreliable or frivolous or plain contrary and other directors might think twice about employing her, regardless of her talent and unblemished track record.

So she must extricate herself in a manner which would maintain some entente even if it was a tad less than cordiale—though how she was going to manage this she did not yet know.

She rose to her feet. 'Let's,' she agreed.

As they set off across the lobby towards the Brierly's renowned and rosetted French restaurant Darcy was conscious of Keir prowling beside her. She was tall and, in her heels, sometimes taller than her escorts, which could be a handicap, but, at six feet four and well-built, he was very much the superior male.

She cast him a sidelong glance. While she half despised herself, his strong presence gave her a curiously protected feeling.

'I wonder whether Maurice has arranged for you to be fed with oysters, followed by asparagus sprinkled with rhino horn?' Keir remarked. 'All washed down by champagne.'

'Excuse me?'

'I got the impression he expects you to be poleaxed by my fatal charm and he might've asked the restaurant to dish up an aphrodisiac or two to help things along.'

'If he has he's wasted his time,' Darcy said pertly.

Keir raised his brows. 'Whatever you eat or drink, you're not going to wrestle me to the ground, drag me beneath the table and have your wicked way with me?'

'And break the first rule in the Brierly's etiquette manual, which is "Do not cause a public scene"? Aw, come *on*.'

He gave the hint of a smile. 'Then how about taking me up to the privacy of my room, perching on my knee, slipping your fingers between the buttons of my shirt and——?'

'No!' Darcy squeaked as images from the past danced like a chorus line of humiliating ghosts before her. She gulped in a breath. 'Out of the question,' she said, biting on every last syllable.

'Pity,' he remarked, and briefly placed a hand between her shoulder blades, where it felt as if it scorched a hole in her jacket. 'After you.'

In the restaurant the *maitre d'* ticked off the booking, which had been made in Maurice's name, and led them to a quiet corner. As they threaded their way between pink-damask-clothed tables, Darcy was aware of a hush in the general buzz of conversation and several discreet glances.

It seemed that either one or perhaps both of them had been recognised, or, regardless of his identity, the interest of the diners had been drawn by Keir's loose-limbed grace. It would be the latter, she decided astringently. His power to incite admiration had always been potent.

'I'm not sure about working with Jed Horwood,' Darcy declared after menus had been read, their choices given, and they were eating cold starters of lobster with mango and curry sauce. She had been searching for an excuse to leave the play, and here she had found one which contained an obliging degree of truth.

'I know he breaks box-office records with his blast-
'em-to-hell pictures, but——' she wrinkled her nose at
the thought of the American macho-man who, after
forging a movie career armed with a Beretta, a forty-
four-inch chest and a mumble, had declared the desire
to 'stretch' himself and appear on stage '—I wonder
whether his talents will transfer.

'So,' Darcy carried on breezily, 'as there's been a
change in director this would seem to be the ideal time
for a change of leading lady. I hate to relinquish the role
but I'm sure you'll agree that it's far better if Jed is
partnered by someone who's one hundred per cent en-
thusiastic about him.'

'You can't pull out,' Keir stated.

Her hackles rose. Her temper began to spark. He
might have been brought in as director and have a special
deal but that did not endow him with the divine right
to dictate what she could or could not do!

'Can't?' she demanded, her nostrils flaring and her
chin tilted belligerently.

'Can't,' he repeated. 'You may have walked out on
me once but you're not going to do it again.'

She frowned. His voice sounded flinty, as though he
had been annoyed about her walking out the first time.
This seemed strange, for she had felt certain that he
would have been relieved, if not downright ecstatic.
Though perhaps Keir had objected to her leaving his
room of her own accord, rather than him ordering her
out. Yes, giving her the old heave-ho—Never darken my
doorstep again, you idiotic and presumptuous child!—
could have appealed to a deep-seated male need to be
the master of every situation.

Darcy glowered. Whatever, she did not appreciate yet
another reminder of the bedroom incident.

'You think so?' she challenged.

'I know so,' he replied. 'You've signed a contract which commits you to play the role, remember?'

'Yes, but as there's been a change of director——'

'Makes no difference. Your name on the dotted line means you agreed to do the job regardless of who directs or of any changes in the cast.' He interrogated her with a look. 'You weren't aware of that?'

'No,' Darcy admitted, cursing herself for her ignorance.

She had been so delighted to be given the role that she had barely skimmed the pages before signing and Maurice had failed to warn her of any clauses which might prove obstructive.

'I've read through everyone's contract,' Keir continued, 'because, frankly, I'm not licking my lips over Jed and you, either. He could pull out in a pinch, but for you it'd be impossible.' He sampled the red burgundy wine which he had chosen. 'Unless, of course, you want to be sued.'

'You mean go through a harrowing court case, be ordered to pay damages, end up broke and destitute?' she enquired acidly. 'I don't.'

'I figured not,' he said.

'How was the lobster?' enquired the waiter, appearing to remove their plates.

Keir smiled. 'Delicious, thank you.'

'Nice,' Darcy muttered, her mind flying every which way.

Just as she had been trapped into dining here with him this evening, so she was trapped into doing the play. She had no option but to work with the director who had had such a crippling effect on her father and never shown one iota of remorse.

Hurt gnawed inside her. One of nature's extroverts, Rupert—he had liked her to call him by his given name— had always brimmed with *joie de vivre*, but after withdrawing from the production he had grown increasingly morose and distracted, until that dreadful day when——

'Lamb cutlets with rosemary for the young lady,' announced the waiter, removing a silver dome with practised flair and setting her plate down in front of her.

Darcy came back to the present. 'Thank you.'

Another dome was expertly flourished. 'And fillet steak, rare, for you, sir.'

As a selection of garden-fresh vegetables was served Darcy's thoughts played hopscotch. Keir had reckoned that he was not licking his lips over either Jed or her? How dared he?

'And what's wrong with *me*?' she demanded, her green eyes glittering. 'Just as you always do a good job of directing, so I always do a good job—no, a *great* job,' she adjusted mutinously, 'of acting.'

Keir looked across at her, then looked up to speak to the waiter. 'Would it be possible for you to bring a sharp knife?' he requested. 'As you can see, my companion is in an inflammatory mood and I have the feeling she'd very much like to cut off my——'

'I don't want to cut off anything,' she gabbled, at speed.

When she had known him before he had sometimes shocked her—and secretly excited her—with his direct approach to matters physical and sexual, and now she was fearful of what he might say. They were dining at the genteel Brierly Hotel, after all.

'That's a relief,' he murmured, and the waiter chuckled. 'Of course,' Keir went on, speaking to the man in a tone of male-bonded confidentiality, 'she's crazy about me really.'

'I am not!' Darcy yelped, then, recognising that he was baiting her and she was falling for it, she shone a plastic smile. 'I think he's cute——'

'Cute?' Keir winced.

'But not *that* cute,' she finished, with crushing relish.

Wary of being baited again, Darcy held back on any further protests until the waiter had safely departed and they were alone.

'You should be grateful that I'm taking the female lead,' she said as she renewed her attack. 'You obviously aren't aware of this but last winter I received an award for the Best Young British Actress of the Year. It's an acknowledgement of outstanding performance given to actresses under thirty and it's been won by a long line of women who are now some of this country's most distinguished actresses.

'I deserved the award,' she went on, with a little puff of self-importance and more than a touch of grandeur, '*and* I was far ahead of the rest of the field.'

'Wowee,' Keir said, placing a fist to his brow in a gesture of mock exultation, but she ignored him.

'I received the award for playing a difficult part in which I was totally realistic and totally convincing, and I've been totally convincing in all the other parts I've done, whether they've been on the stage or on television. My stage credits have included...'

As she catalogued a trio of West End successes Darcy listened to herself in surprise. She had been grossly sceptical of the award, as she was of all acting awards, yet this evening she had flaunted it. Also, mention the word 'publicity' and normally she cringed, yet now she was publicising herself and doing an excellent job.

Maybe she could be accused of going over the top, but it could not be helped. What mattered was making Keir realise, and acknowledge, that in her he had a jewel, a veritable *diamond*.

'And ever since I won the award scripts have been thudding through my letter box, including some from Hollywood film producers,' she informed him in a voice which thumbed her nose and said, So there! 'Maurice is urging me to grab the scripts with two sweaty hands,' Darcy went on, then hesitated, frowning. 'How-ever——'

'I know about your award,' Keir interrupted, as though her hard sell had exhausted his patience and any more would have had him stampeding hysterically for the door. 'I also saw the play and was impressed.'

'You did?' she said in surprise. 'You were?'

'Most impressed.'

Coming from a director of his clout, this was praise indeed—but Darcy refused to blubber her thanks or even smile. Instead she coolly tossed the drift of dark curls back from her shoulders. 'So you should've been,' she said.

Keir had started to eat and he nodded towards her plate. 'Don't let your meal go cold.'

Obediently she picked up her knife and fork and for a few minutes they ate in silence. 'So why aren't you happy with either Jed or me?' she demanded, when her lamb cutlets had been reduced to bone. 'I'm——'

'A phenomenal actress. Message received and under-stood.' His look was sardonic. 'But I didn't say Jed or you—my reference was to Jed *and* you together. Have you met the guy?' She shook her head. 'I have and——' He broke off. 'How tall are you?'

'Five feet nine.'

'He's much the same, in his built-up heels. But the male lead's height is important because it's integral to the plot that he's seen to physically dominate the girl. Some actors—good stage actors—could create the illusion despite the lack of inches, but Jed? I doubt it.

'He's also dark and so are you, but a visual contrast would be better. The two characters are supposed to be chalk and cheese, different in many ways, until finally they join together.' He eyed her sable-brown curls. 'I couldn't persuade you to get busy with the bleach bottle?'

'Persuade?' Darcy said warily. 'Going platinum isn't stipulated in my contract?'

'Nope.'

She expelled a sigh of relief. As soon as she could she would go through the small print with a fine-tooth comb. 'Then no chance.'

'I don't blame you,' Keir said, and, stretching an arm across the table, he entwined a wisp of her hair around a long finger. 'You have beautiful hair.'

'Thanks,' Darcy said, and drew back, forcing him to draw back too. She knew that it was simply his charm kicking in and her common sense kicking out, yet his touch seemed alarmingly intimate. Like a lover's touch. 'So you have your doubts about Jed's capabilities too?' she enquired.

Keir nodded. 'Between you and me, I feel that in insisting on taking on the role he's being overly ambitious. By far. That said, I'll squeeze as good a performance as it's possible to get out of the guy and I won't let him turn the play into a piece of hokum.

'However,' he added, with a faintly mocking twist to his mouth, 'while I hesitate to step on your ego—or put myself at risk of an impromptu vasectomy—don't forget that it's Jed who'll bring in the audiences. You might be the cat's pyjamas of the British stage but in the States you're an unknown.'

Aware of being adroitly cut down to size, Darcy gave a thin smile. 'True.'

'Though,' he continued, 'there are some who'll recognise you as Sir Rupert Weston's daughter.'

She shot him a glance. His expression looked benign but did she detect condemnation again or could this be a jibe? From the start of her career Darcy had had to face comments, sometimes envious, sometimes scathing, about how she was following in her father's footsteps, yet doing so had not been easy. His fame was a double-edged sword in that while it had opened some doors it had closed others; and on the occasions when she had got inside she had had to perform and expectations had been high.

'True,' she repeated, being determinedly noncommittal. 'Why did you agree to direct the play if you have doubts about Jed Horwood?' she enquired, when they had both refused dessert but ordered coffee.

'Because it's so cleverly plotted and the dialogue crackles with such credible passions that, given dedicated performances, it has the ability to be theatrical dynamite. And because my financial deal is excellent.'

'It is?' she said, with a frown.

He nodded. 'I had something going which I was reluctant to leave, but a special deal whereby I get a percentage of the profits was hammered out and I agreed,' he explained. He swirled the remaining red wine in his glass. 'I also agreed because the rehearsals and previews take place in Washington.'

'What's special about that?'

'I live in Washington.'

'I didn't know,' Darcy said, thinking that in fact she knew very little about his private life.

'In Georgetown, so it means I'll be able to keep a handle on—the rest of my activities,' he said vaguely, 'which is useful.'

His activities? What did he mean? she wondered, and it suddenly occurred to her that her one-time hero could now have a wife and it might be family life which demanded his attention. A line cut between her brows. The idea shocked and oddly jarred.

'Are you married?' she enquired.

'No,' he replied a little brusquely.

'Oh, I just thought that, well, your looks and your talent make you quite a catch——'

'You're not praising me?' Keir drawled when she stopped, aware of talking herself into an awkward verbal corner.

'And you're thirty-six, which is a marriageable age,' Darcy finished in a rush.

'I'm still single,' he said, and raised his glass in a toast. 'Here's to the success of the play and here's to the next time we meet—in Washington in a fortnight.'

'A fortnight? You mean in a month,' she protested.

'No. This appears to be something else which Maurice neglected to mention,' Keir said mordantly, 'but rehearsals start in two weeks' time. As you know, the lead roles are complex and, while Bill Shapiro may've been happy with a month of rehearsals overall, I'm not. I want two weeks with you and Jed working on the script together and alone before the rest of the cast arrives. OK?'

'Do I have a choice?' Darcy enquired tartly.

A grin tugged at the corner of his mouth and he shook his head. 'None,' he said.

CHAPTER TWO

FASCINATED by the panorama which stretched for miles into the hazy, shimmering distance, Darcy gazed out of the tenth-floor window. As her eyes travelled across rooftops, traffic-dotted streets and swaths of green to focus on the dome of the Capitol, gleaming in the afternoon sunshine, she smiled. This was her first time in Washington and her plane had only touched down a couple of hours ago, yet already she was enchanted.

'Jim-dandy city, ain't it?' the friendly black cab driver had said, noticing her pleasure on the journey in from the airport, and she had assured him that with wide boulevards, majestic memorials and squint-white obelisks Washington lived up to its claim of being the greatest free show on earth.

Her focus blurred. Enchantment was not a feature on her agenda; she had come here to work—with Keir Robards.

Although at first she had raged against what had seemed the inscrutable, star-crossed perversity of fate, over the past fortnight she had gradually come to realise that, by throwing them together, fate had performed a favour, insomuch as it had presented her with two opportunities. The first was to be a smash hit in the play, for, in all honesty, Keir's directing abilities by far exceeded those of Bill Shapiro, and the second was to get even.

Darcy tweaked at the neck of the putty-coloured silk top which she wore with matching trousers. No, not

30

even—full retribution could never be exacted—but she would make it plain that while Keir might have trampled mercilessly over her father he could not trample over her—and she would take some revenge in the process.

She was not malicious by nature, but she did not see why he should escape from his sins scot-free, not now that fate had so emphatically intervened and when her relationship with Keir Robards was beginning to seem more and more like unfinished business. She might have thought about him spasmodically, yet it had not been *so* spasmodic and she had never forgotten him. How could she have done when he had had such a dramatic effect on her life—in different ways?

Darcy nibbled pensively at a fingernail. She must not do anything which might damage her reputation or mar the play—that would be counterproductive—but whenever a chance arose to rile, unsettle or alarm the man she would take it. For the next couple of months she intended to make Keir Robards' life hell—subtly.

Her thought-train jumped tracks. What were the activities on which he wanted to keep 'a handle'? Darcy wondered. She had been wondering about this and his reference to having 'something going' which he was reluctant to leave. Could Keir have been unwilling to be separated from a lover who shared his Washington home, and, as the separation while they were in New York would not be too lengthy, was that why he had eventually agreed? It seemed feasible. Who was his live-in lover?

Abruptly Darcy swung from the window. She had better things to do than speculate over Keir's personal affairs, which did not interest her anyway. Her unpacking awaited, after which she would ring her new boss—oh, how the prospect of being bossed by him rankled—and advise him of her arrival.

She was in an impressive city and staying at a spectacular hotel, Darcy reflected as she hung up her clothes. An architectural marvel of bronze girders and tinted glass, the De Robillard was, so Maurice, who had fixed the accommodation, had informed her, the most prestigious hotel in town.

Her eyes travelled across the chic taupe and white quilted emperor-size bed, the vast walls of wardrobes, the mirrored bar with its mind-boggling selection of on-the-house drinks. It also had to be one of the most spacious.

After she had walked what seemed like miles, putting everything away, Darcy lifted the onyx telephone and dialled Keir's number.

'It's Darcy,' she said when he answered. 'I've arrived and I'm installed.'

'Installed where?'

'At the De Robillard.'

There was a moment of silence. 'How's the jet lag?' he enquired.

'Non-existent.'

'Then how about bringing over your script and we can make a start?'

'Now?' she said in surprise.

'Now.'

Darcy dithered. Last night, anticipation of needing to be up before dawn in order to catch her flight—and an itchy awareness of seeing Keir again—had meant that her sleep had been fitful. Which, in turn, meant that, while she felt wide awake at this moment, she could slump without warning. So should she backtrack, plead incipient weariness and hope to annoy—or did she show him that she was a professional? Demonstrating her professionalism won.

'You want me to come to a rehearsal hall?' she asked.

'I want you to come to my home. The journey won't take long in a cab.'

Darcy reached for her caramel-coloured suede jacket. Forget the refreshing soak in the Jacuzzi that you had planned, she thought. Forget a stop at the hotel's marble-pillared coffee-shop. Forget a stroll outside to view the White House.

'What's the address?' she enquired.

When she met Keir this time she would be cool and composed, Darcy told herself as the cab sped along the busy city roads. A fortnight ago, being faced with him out of the blue had thrown her and, like the teenager she had once been, she had racketed around from blushes to squeaks to gabbles. But forewarned was forearmed and now, whatever Keir might say or do, she refused to be fazed. As for him attracting her...

Once more Darcy chewed at her fingernail. Because there was no man currently in her life, she supposed that she was what was described as sex-starved, and thus susceptible. However, by reacting to Keir, her hormones had acted the traitor. From now on they would be kept under strict control, but if they should react to him again she would ignore them.

At the driver's comment that they were entering Georgetown, Darcy peered eagerly out of the window. According to an article in the airline magazine which she had read on the plane, this was one of the District of Columbia's most fashionable neighbourhoods. It boasted late eighteenth- and nineteenth-century homes, where high-society hostesses entertained luminaries from the diplomatic and political worlds, interesting shops and myriad fine restaurants.

Refined and yet vibrant with vitality, Georgetown was a desirable residential urban village, something like an American version of Hampstead, Darcy decided.

The address that Keir had provided turned out to be a gracious turn-of-the-century brick villa on a quiet, leafy street. She walked up the short drive, mounted a flight of stone steps to a white-glossed front door, and pressed the bell. Hastily finger-combing her hair, Darcy adopted an expression which was intended to portray both maturity and sang-froid.

'Hi,' Keir said as the front door swung open.

In close-fitting jeans and a navy open-necked shirt which revealed a smattering of dark blond hair in the V at his throat, he looked all male, all lean physique, all powerful. Seeing him again hit her like a blow somewhere between the solar plexus and the upper thigh.

Darcy snatched in a breath. She was not going to be fazed? Her hormones would be controlled or, at least, ignored? Wrong on each count. The idea had been a huge folly. Her brow furrowed. Yet to be attracted to a man whom she classed as an enemy was a skewed notion which indicated a troublesome schizophrenia.

'Hello,' she said, the word emerging irritatingly like a gasp.

Keir smiled the kind of smile which once she would have drowned in. 'Come in. Let me take your jacket,' he said, and hitched it up amid a row of his which hung on brass hooks.

'Has Jed Horwood arrived yet?' she whispered furtively as he ushered her through a hall with stained-glass windows and a grandfather clock, and into an airy living-room.

'No, he——'

'Good, because I want to ask you something before he does. Last week I rented out videos of several of his films and now, frankly, acting with His Machoness is beginning to seem more and more a dubious pleasure,' she said, arrowing in on a third worry which had helped to keep her awake the previous night.

'I know you promised to get the best out of him, but, after seeing how wooden he is, I doubt if he *has* any best. Not only that but the celluloid Jed Horwood is so brash and smug.' Darcy pulled a face. 'Seriously awful.

'I realise that he might be different in the flesh, but if not it could be a dampener. His character and mine are supposed to feel an irresistible urge for each other and, while I'm perfectly capable of acting this out——' the declaration was defiant '—it would help if Jed Horwood weren't a jerk. So,' she demanded, reaching the end of her hurried spiel, 'please would you tell me what the real man is like?'

'In a word——' Keir pursed his lips '—obnoxious.'

'I knew it!' Darcy wailed. 'In that case it's going to take——'

He cut her off. 'We'll talk about Jed in a minute. Can I get you a coffee?'

'Oh—please.'

'Cream?' he enquired, gesturing to her to come with him through an archway and into the kitchen.

'Just a dash.'

As he lifted a bubbling percolator Darcy put her thoughts about Jed Horwood on hold and gazed around. Fitted in limed oak and equipped with state-of-the-art appliances, the kitchen was streamlined yet cosy.

Her eyes strayed back to the pale-carpeted living-room, to a cauliflower-check sofa, to a wall unit which held television and stereo, to green and white curtains which floated at the sash windows. Although elegant, like its owner, the decor was a little spartan for her taste, but the room was light, well-shaped and possessed potential.

'I like your house,' she said.

'Thanks. The place was virtually falling apart when I bought it a few years ago and since then I've spent a lot of time abroad, so I'm still in the process of getting things how I want them.'

'Abroad where?' she asked.

'South America, the Caribbean, and I was in India for three months earlier this year.'

So he spent the time between assignments on holiday. This surprised her for, no matter how fascinating the locations were, Keir seemed too active and vigorous an individual to swan around for quite so long.

'Sugar?' he enquired.

Darcy shook her head. 'Don't take it.'

Her gaze returned to the living-room. Unlike the homes of some entertainment people which she had visited, there were no silver-framed photographs showing him arm in arm with Hollywood megastars, no cavalcade of posters which advertised his productions and proclaimed his success to every passing visitor, no evidence of the awards she knew he had won. While she was reluctant to give praise, he did seem to have his place in the world in a pleasingly modest perspective.

'Where are your trophies?' she asked.

'In a cupboard somewhere,' he replied, and cast her a wry look. 'You have your Best Actress statuette slap bang in the middle of the mantlepiece, highly polished and spotlit at night?'

'Wrong! It's also in a cupboard.'

He gazed at her in silence for a moment, then he opened the fridge. 'I guess an apartment would've been easier to run than a house,' he reflected, 'but I like space.' Keir returned the cream-jug to a shelf. 'So do you,' he said.

'Me?'

'I understand the bedrooms at the De Robillard are the size of aircraft hangars.'

Darcy grinned at his description. 'Almost. My bedroom at home would fit three times into the room I've been given and twice into the bathroom,' she told him, 'which, in addition to all the usual facilities, has a Jacuzzi and a multi-purpose exercise machine.'

Standing with his long legs apart, Keir folded tanned arms across his chest. 'And you figure that as an award-winning, big-shot actress you deserve nothing but the best?'

Her grin withered. The cobalt-blue eyes were critical and so was his tone. Darcy knew that back in London she had been over-zealous with the airs and graces, but now they had begun to rebound.

'No, I don't and it wasn't my idea to——' She swerved. 'You're thinking how my father liked to live in the lap of luxury and that I'm the same?' Darcy demanded. 'You're mistaken. I'm not. But if he enjoyed driving around in Rolls-Royces and drinking fine brandies and cruising the Mediterranean on fancy yachts, so what? An appetite for good living is not a crime and even if it did mean he died penniless it——'

'Rupert hadn't crossed my mind,' Keir said. He fixed her with piercing blue eyes. 'But you seem knotted up about him.'

'Rubbish,' Darcy rejected sharply, and frowned. Her outburst had surprised her as much as it had obviously surprised him, and she had no idea where it had come from, no idea what had made her veer off into a spontaneous defence of her father or even mention him. It was, after all, a personal and disconcerting area.

Darcy readjusted her grip on the bulky pale blue bound copy of the script which she held to her chest. She was not going to attempt to explain or excuse herself—even if she could. 'Carry on,' she instructed.

'Thanks,' Keir said grittily. 'Have you any idea how much staying at the De Robillard during your two months or so in Washington will cost?'

'Er...none.'

All she knew was that the production company was picking up the tab. Should she tell him that Maurice had chosen the hotel and it had not occurred to her to query it? How she had simply assumed that the choice had been sanctioned? Darcy hesitated. But, if she did, once again she would appear to have left too much to her clever-dick agent and once again she would appear incompetent.

'But you don't care. Well, you may not give a damn about soaking the system and sending the expenses for the production shooting into orbit but *I* do,' Keir rasped, and he brought his hand down flat on a worktop like the blade of a wide knife, making her jump. 'As someone who's to receive a share of the profits I intend to see that we make a profit and that it's not frittered away by——' he jabbed a finger '—*you.*'

Darcy's chin lifted. She objected to being accused and so roundly denounced. She also refused to be heaped with all the blame.

'And by Jed Horwood,' she said.

'What?'

'If my accommodation is five-star his must be even more so,' she declared, for the movie actor's taste for the perks and privileges of stardom was notorious. 'I've heard how on film sets he demands an elaborately de-signed trailer and expects his every wish to be met by a sizeable and fawning entourage, who are known as "doormats" because he likes to walk over them.

'So while Jed's in Washington he'll doubtless be par-ading it in a super de luxe penthouse somewhere, with a coterie of servants, including a chauffeur and a chef and a personal fitness trainer, to look after him.'

Keir shook his head. 'No,' he said impatiently.

'All right, Jed Horwood has rented a mansion,' Darcy said, charging straight into an alternative scenario. 'With a billiard-room and a swimming-pool, and a stretch limo waiting in the drive. And——'

'While I hesitate to stop you in full flow,' he said sar-donically, 'not that either. We're working in the study,' he told her, and, picking up the steaming mug of coffee, he strode off.

Darcy hesitated; then, left with no other option but to trail in his wake, she followed. She glared at his broad, navy-shirted back. Her espadrilles were flat, which meant that today she was several inches shorter. Today she did not feel protected by his presence; today she felt sub-ordinate. Trifling. Small fry. Big man and the little woman, Darcy thought sourly as Keir led the way to a room at the back of the house. A big man with a neat rear end, muscled thighs and long legs, the hormonal part of her mind added.

To one side of the study stood a desk, bearing a tele-phone and computer, a swivel chair and a trio of filing cabinets, while the other half of the room contained a comfy chintz-covered ottoman and a glass-topped coffee-table. Three walls were lined floor to ceiling with books, while large windows in the fourth looked on to a garden, where sunlight dappled a patio and a lawn encircled with spring-green trees.

Placing her script on the table, Darcy sat down. A budding home-maker, she always took an interest in other people's houses and if this one were hers she would, she decided, put leafy pot plants on shelves and window-sills and bring the spirit of the garden indoors.

'Thank you,' she said, accepting the mug which Keir handed to her. She took a sip of coffee. 'So where is Jed Horwood staying?' she asked a mite tetchily.

'He isn't.' Swinging his chair round to face her, he levered his long body down into it. 'He's quit the production.'

Stunned, Darcy looked at him. 'Crikey.'

'Succinctly put.'

'But—but the play's still on?' she faltered, struggling to absorb this latest item of shock news and make the necessary mental adjustments. 'It is,' she said, answering her own question, for Keir had summoned her here in order for them to make a start. 'I'm relieved that Jed's gone—extremely—but——' she was intrigued and a little apprehensive '—who's playing the male lead now?'

Keir stretched out his denim-clad legs, leaned back in the swivel chair and gave an idle swing. 'I am.'

She stared. Her whole stomach turned over. For a moment she was on the brink of yelping, squeaking and screaming a protest—You can't, you mustn't, *no*!—but in the next she remembered how she would not—repeat *not*—be fazed.

She drew in an unsteady breath. She had been right to feel apprehensive, but Keir was joking, using a devilish black humour to tease her...wasn't he?

'You?' she said, without expression but with a great deal of care.

His lips curved into a wry smile. 'Life's a bitch, isn't it?'

Darcy sat as if carved from ice. This was no joke. Keir Robards playing the male lead, playing opposite her, was fact—chill, hard, entrapping fact.

'You wouldn't be my first choice,' she said tautly, and could not resist adding, 'Nor my last.'

'But you'll rise to the occasion?' he enquired, and his voice carried the hint of a dare.

Her eyes glittered. 'Like a rocket,' she informed him.

'I must remember to stand well back when you light the blue touch-paper,' he said drily.

'It would be advisable,' she responded. Darcy took a drink of coffee, though a stiff whisky would have done a better job of calming her nerves. 'Why you?' she asked.

'Cal Warburg, who I assume you know is head of the production company——'

'I do. I'm not that unaware,' she protested.

'Relieved to hear it. Anyway, Cal felt it'd be impossible to find another movie star of anywhere near equivalent fame at such short notice,' he continued, 'and as I'm still remembered as an actor he approached me. He reckons that my appeal, such as it is, will draw in sufficient punters to keep the production viable.' He frowned. 'Personally, I feel it's a high-risk situation.'

Darcy looked him dead in the eyes. 'Me too.' Mr Warburg might play the flattery game but she preferred to tell the truth—and if Keir was offended, tough! 'And let us not forget,' she continued, 'that as it's a long time since you acted——'

'Five years.'

'—you might also be rusty.' Darcy shone a see-through smile. 'Very.'

'While Jed Horwood may not be the worst actor in the world, he comes close,' Keir said, unruffled by her barb. 'So no matter how out of practice I am I'll still be a darn sight better. However,' he went on, 'if I'd refused to do the part the play would've been pulled.'

'You expect me to be abjectly grateful?' she demanded.

'And sink down before me on your knees to perform an act of worship? That won't be necessary.' He slid his hands into his trouser pockets—an action which pulled the denim tight across his thighs and made her searingly aware of his masculinity, and conscious of a sexual innuendo. 'Unless, of course, you're eager to express your appreciation in such a way?'

'I'm not.'

A dark blond brow arched. 'You might like it.'

'Wish on,' Darcy retorted, and he laughed.

Being directed by Keir had been hard enough to swallow, but now she was expected to act with him! Nervousness quivered in the pit of her stomach. The play's basic storyline revolved around the two main characters splitting up, meeting again and going through the trauma of making up. This included clinches, kisses, and reached its climax in a scene of highly charged passion when his character overpowered hers. On a bed.

Darcy's nervousness spiralled into blind panic. Her errant hormones meant that there had to be a million pitfalls in the physical intimacy which was demanded. Could she cope? No. Yes. No. She must; she had no choice.

A breath was taken. 'And to persuade you Mr Warburg designed an even handsomer financial package?' Darcy asked.

'He did. He made me an offer which I couldn't refuse.'

Her smile was frosty. 'While I'm doing the role for a pittance.'

'You are,' Keir acknowledged, 'but you're also doing the role because it fulfils a dream.'

'Dream? What dream?' she demanded.

'The dream Rupert had. Although he would've dearly loved to work on Broadway he never managed to get there, so he pinned all his hopes on you, his cherished only child. And if he's looking down from heaven when we open there I have no doubt he'll be bursting with parental pride.'

Darcy shot him a suspicious look. Was Keir being snide or mocking? Neither. His remarks had been the straightforward truth as he saw it.

She took another mouthful of coffee. But what was *her* truth? Although she could well remember her father telling her how thrilled he would be if, one day, she were to appear on Broadway, she had not been consciously aware of aiming to fulfil his expectations.

And yet, while her role was undoubtedly a prime one, in addition to the low salary there were other aspects which had troubled her—like the high sexual content and a demand for partial nudity. These concerns had been brushed aside, but would she have brushed them aside if the production was to have been staged in London? Her winged brows lowered. She suspected not. She suspected that they could have proved a stumbling block.

Darcy sighed. She had never analysed what had motivated her to rush headlong to do the play, but now her father's hopes seemed to have been the major influence—although an unconscious one. So how should she answer Keir? Should she admit to the truth and attempt to defend what seemed to be flawed reasoning, or should she lie through her teeth?

Looking across at him, she saw that no answer was required for just as she had been engrossed in her thoughts, so was he.

'I'm not sure whether or not I made the right decision,' Keir muttered, rubbing contemplative fingers back and forth along the hard edge of his jaw.

'Why's that?'

'Because I'd decided never to act again.'

Darcy lanced him with a look. 'And that's because you prefer to order other people around,' she said, recalling the remark he had made at the Brierly, but turning it into a denunciation. 'Because you enjoy being in charge and cracking the whip.'

'You make me sound like a control freak,' he protested.

'You're not?' she challenged.

Keir shook his head. 'I set high standards for myself and for those I work with, so I admit that the whip does get cracked on occasion—but only when it's necessary. Although I used to get a buzz out of acting a role and getting it right,' he went on, 'I find being a director far more satisfying. And it does have one significant plus,' he added, as if talking to himself.

The plus would be money, Darcy thought acidly. For actors, the super-lavish pay-days came from making films, not from working on the stage as Keir had done in the main, though he had appeared in one or two low-budget films. Yet, given full-house audiences, his current percentage deal could be lucrative. And top-notch film directors could command million-dollar fees.

'But the lure of a big fat cheque overcame your better judgement?' she enquired.

A muscle clenched in his jaw. Keir clearly resented her charge and for a moment seemed about to justify himself—how? she wondered—but then he shrugged. 'I guess. In addition to rescuing you from Jed Horwood's acting, my taking over also saves you from another fate worse than death,' he said, as if feeling a requirement to redeem himself in some kind of way. 'Having to hang out with the guy.'

'How hang out?' Darcy questioned.

'Going drinking with him and his cronies until the wee small hours, or being expected to put in lengthy attendances in his dressing-room while he regales you with monologues on what a marvellous human being he is, or maybe even sleeping with him.'

'Sleeping with him?' she repeated. 'My behaviour may have been...less than circumspect once upon a time——'

'Nice turn of phrase,' Keir inserted.

'—but you can't believe I'm *that* easy?' Darcy protested indignantly. 'Surely you don't consider me to be a tramp like some of Jed Horwood's past partners? Or a nymphomaniac?' she asked, and gave a terse, inward laugh. If only he knew the reality.

'I don't,' Keir replied equably. 'However, you must've heard how the guy takes it for granted that he'll bed each of his leading ladies, if not every other actress in the cast?'

'I have, but he wouldn't have bedded me.' A picture of the star's self-satisfied swagger and oily smile swam before her. 'Jed Horwood would not have laid one finger on me,' Darcy declared forcefully.

'Not like I did,' Keir murmured, and his blue eyes tangled with hers, 'when you were a virgin.'

CHAPTER THREE

A TIDE of hot colour swept up her face. Seven years melted away and, once again, Darcy was back in Keir's bedroom at the Brierly Hotel, sitting on his knee in her low-cut dress and shamelessly flirting. As she had slid her fingers inside his shirt and touched the curls of coarse hair on his chest he had stroked her breasts.

At the memory she felt her nipples pinch and tighten. She was aware of that blissful ache. Abruptly Darcy remembered the silky top that she was wearing and how it clung like a second skin to her body. Ye gods, Keir wouldn't notice her flagrant nipples, would he?

'What makes you so sure that I was a virgin?' she demanded, needing to talk, needing to say something—anything—which would keep his eyes focused on her face.

'You had an untouched quality, a demureness which curiously——' he hesitated, frowning '—despite Gideon McCall *et al*, you still retain.'

Darcy's heart lurched. She would ignore the first and last alarmingly perceptive parts of his remark and concentrate on the middle.

'*Et al*?' she protested. 'Like most girls in their twenties, over the past few years I've had boyfriends, and because I'm an actress and the daughter of someone well-known my relationships have been written about in the Press.' She frowned. 'Much to my regret. However, they've been lightweight and short-lived and not,' Darcy insisted, with some heat, 'the succession of steamy affairs which you seem to imply.'

His eyes flickered over her in an unfathomable look. 'You're not a compulsive sexual adventurer like your father?'

'No. Did Maurice know that Jed Horwood had pulled out of the play?' she enquired.

Keir hoisted a brow. 'How come you're not leaping to Rupert's defence?'

'It's difficult to defend someone who was married three times and who had numerous mistresses,' Darcy replied stiffly.

'You reckon he overdid the romantic side of life?'

She gave a razor of a smile. When journalists quizzed her about her father it always made her uneasy and she objected to his questioning now. 'A little,' she said.

'Maurice didn't know,' he said, belatedly answering her enquiry, 'because Jed only contacted Cal Warburg late yesterday. Seems he'd had second thoughts about acting without access to multiple takes and had gone into a blue funk. Which caused much gnashing of teeth and banging of heads at the offices of the Warburg empire, though in my opinion the guy made a wise career move. And in my opinion,' he went on, 'we'll do well together.'

As she thought again about the kisses, the clinches, the body-on-body contact which their roles demanded, Darcy's heartbeat accelerated. Once she would have revelled in such a chance to partake in legitimate intimacy but now it made her quake.

'Because you'll dominate me?' she asked, striving to sound matter-of-fact and not like a gibbering wreck. 'Because you're fair and I'm dark?'

'Both of those, but also because there's a sexual attraction between us.'

She looked at him in alarm. What was he saying? Had he noticed the jut of her nipples lifting the fine silk and recognised her susceptibility? Did he sense that her hormones could not be trusted?

'There is not!' Darcy flared, using attack as the best form of defence.

'No?'

'*No.*'

Keir moved his shoulders. 'OK, I'll rephrase that—because there *was* a sexual attraction between us.'

Darcy leant forward and, needing to steady a hand which was infuriatingly shaky, set her empty coffee-mug down on the table. While she was relieved by his use of the past tense, his memory was defective. 'Between' had not existed; the attraction had been on one side only—hers.

Keir might have thought she was pretty and had doubtless been flattered by her adoring teenage interest, but as far as real, intense, driving-him-wild attraction was concerned it had not happened. He had been fleetingly tempted by the allure of her cleavage, but that was all. The whetting of his physical appetite had been minimal and her impact on his emotions had been zero. Darcy knew that she ought to point out these brutal facts and deny his assertion, but a foolish pride held her mute.

'And because we have that sexual history,' Keir continued, 'we must use it in the play.'

She gave a lame smile and once again said nothing.

Pushing himself up from the chair, he took a copy of the script from his desk and came to sit beside her. 'How do you see your character?' he enquired.

Grateful to be allowed to escape from the tensions of the here and now and enter a pretend world, Darcy swiftly reorganised her thoughts. After reading through the script several times, she had formed an interpretation, though she had not put it into words.

'To me, Anna is an enchanting yet egocentric rich girl,' she began tentatively, 'who, until she came up against Marcus, had always done whatever she wanted and never worried about the consequences. She's headstrong with a touch of wildness, and because of that she's landed herself in some dubious situations, like the ill-considered affair she rushed into when they were apart.'

Keir nodded. 'I agree, plus I'd add that she's emotionally fragile.'

She moved her hand in a swift, negative karate chop. 'She's tough!'

'Fragile and vulnerable.'

'You're nuts!'

'Perhaps,' he said mildly, 'but Cal Warburg told me that the reason his London casting director was so insistent that you play the part was that he felt you have a touching air of vulnerability. And you do.'

Darcy uttered a rude word.

'OK, it's a deceptive air,' Keir remarked drolly, 'because we both know that behind the fine bone-structure and limpid green eyes there lives the soul of an assault commander. But you're playing Anna because Anna can be, and is, wounded.'

'Wounded, but only slightly and temporarily, because Anna has grit.'

'Deeply wounded,' he said.

'Nonsense on stilts!' she declared.

Although she genuinely believed in the authenticity of her reading of her character, as they disagreed Darcy

realised that she had found an opportunity to rile and
unsettle him—and her ideas about Anna went further.

'You know how, in the stage directions, Marcus ties
her wrists to the headboard in the final act?' she said.
'Anna would never submit to that. She's a modern girl,
and modern girls just don't accept that kind of
Neanderthal behaviour.'

'You mean *you* don't accept it?' Keir enquired, making
the question personal.

Darcy looked at him with startled eyes. 'What kind
of sexual activities do you think I go in for?' she
protested.

'Be it whips and chains, Kama Sutra antics or hanging
from a helicopter by your teeth, whatever you get up to
is your choice,' he said silkily. 'However, I assume from
your reaction that no one's attempted to tie you to a
bed.'

'Never.'

'In that case why don't we give it a try?' In a single,
fluid movement, Keir turned and captured her wrists in
two large hands. 'Why don't we go upstairs and discover
whether my "Neanderthal behaviour" is unacceptable
or——' his voice took on a seductive huskiness '—if it
gives you one heck of a thrill?'

Darcy's heart began to hammer. Place and time faded,
and her only awareness was of the blue eyes looking deep
into hers and the grip of the strong fingers which seemed
to burn like a brand on her flesh.

Keep calm, she ordered herself. Stay cool. Keir's
baiting you again. And yet some time in the not too
distant future they would need to block out the physical
action of the play. Some time they would have to or-
chestrate the moves on the bed and lie there together.
The hammering of her heart increased. Some time, Darcy

thought, making a frantic clutch for comfort, but not today.

'Interesting idea, but it isn't my reaction that counts, it's Anna's,' she said in a determinedly light tone. 'And I know she'd never agree.'

Keir's brows came down low. 'You're suggesting we should scrub the tying?' he demanded.

'I am. It's not stated precisely in the text, so——'

'It's what the writer intended.'

'How do you know?' Darcy protested. 'The writer's dead. He died just weeks after completing the manuscript.'

'I'm alert to the nuances. But whatever the guy intended it's still a dramatic piece of theatre,' he insisted, and, with his interest now focused entirely on the play, he released her, much to her relief. 'It not only symbolises that Marcus has also managed to capture Anna emotionally, which is the whole point of the scene, but it's a visual image which the audience'll take home, remember and *think about*.'

'Anna wouldn't let it happen,' Darcy said stubbornly. 'And the feminists will have the vapours.'

'Their problem,' Keir grated, and skewered her with a look. 'You're not planning on being a problem to me, are you?'

Her tongue circled over her lips. She knew that he was clever, but she had not expected him to home in on her intentions quite so quickly. If at all.

'A problem?' she repeated, dissembling and playing for time.

'You're not trying to provoke a fight?'

Darcy smiled, the embodiment of sweet reasonableness. 'Whatever makes you say that?'

'I wonder,' he said darkly. 'But let me give you a warning—don't.'

At the rasping word she frowned. Her father must have been a problem to him and suffered in consequence but a problem how? On Rupert's withdrawal from the production, which had been at the very last minute, he and Keir had issued a joint Press statement saying that they had agreed to differ. That was all. No explanation had been given nor had either man criticised the other. On the surface it had been an amicable, if puzzling parting of the ways.

Yet only on the surface, for, while her father had sturdily maintained a carefree public persona, in private he had been introspective. And when she had asked him what had happened he had refused point-blank to talk about it. Like his introspection, this had been out of character. Rupert had never been able to resist telling a story even in confidence and even against himself, so his silence had been proof that far from being a conflict of opinion over how his role should be played, which was the reason Darcy had originally settled on, the truth behind the split was murkier.

Up to that point she had seen nothing bad about Keir Robards. Despite the bedroom incident and some uncharitable observations from his girlfriend, Suzanne, perhaps she had even hoped that he might belatedly realise he was ablaze with love for her and arrive to stake claim. But as Rupert had grown increasingly depressed the idea that Keir might possess a sinister side had taken hold.

With his work methods, could he have acted the tyrant and deliberately destroyed her father's confidence—a confidence which had always seemed of the tough-as-old-boots variety? Had getting the better of a man so much older and of such fame been a sadistic exhibition of muscle-flexing?

She had heard no rumours, nor talk of Keir acting the tyrant before or since, though, not wanting to whinge and fearing his reprisal, people might have preferred to remain silent. Yet something had happened in their collaboration which had turned Rupert into a tortured soul. *What* had happened? For seven years Darcy had lived with a head full of questions, but over the next few weeks she intended to find the answers.

As she looked at Keir she braced her shoulders. Whatever he threw at her—violent moods, fits of temper—she would not be tyrannised. Though he did not even need to be moody or bad-tempered; tyranny came in all sorts of guises and his could be more insidious and far more destructive than most.

'You aren't interested in my ideas?' she asked coolly.

'On the contrary, I'm extremely interested, and if you can convince me that they're right and add to the play I'll be more than happy to go along with them. But——' his blue eyes were slaty '——I don't like people wasting my time and giving me the run-around. Get the picture?'

'Wide screen,' Darcy replied, yet although her retort was snappy she felt a tremor of trepidation. In attempting to rile him she would be entering dangerous territory, but she was determined to make him pay a penance for her father's sake. 'The play was originally seen as something of a showcase for Jed Horwood,' she said, trying a different tack, 'and, while his tying up a woman might have seemed credible, he's gone.'

'You don't reckon me tying up a woman is credible?' Keir enquired.

Darcy gave a strained smile. She considered it entirely so. He might possess style and elegance—qualities which Jed sorely lacked—but his steely machismo made him all man. Although she had not seen him act on stage she had watched his films, so she knew that if Keir was required to ditch ten thousand years of civilisation and become the savage he could do it.

As she visualised the erotic sexual image of him tying her to the bed her pulses started to race. But *he* would not tie *her*—it was Marcus who tied Anna, she reminded herself. She moistened lips which had gone dry. In her mind they were entangled and it was difficult to separate the two.

'I'm sure it would be credible,' Darcy said, and took a breath. 'However——'

'Let's leave the tying scene for now,' Keir said curtly, 'and discuss it another day.'

'Whatever you wish,' she said, and smiled. She might not have won the war but, by irritating him, she had won a battle, albeit a small one. 'One more point I'd like to raise——'

His jaw tightened. 'Only one?'

'——concerns Anna taking off her nightgown in the earlier scene, being naked beneath the sheet which she wraps around her when she gets out of bed to talk to Marcus, and briefly revealing her breasts. I'm not happy with it.'

'You're not playing the scene to be happy, you're playing it to be effective,' he told her.

'Even so, I don't consider the nudity necessary.'

'Since when have you become a shrinking violet?' Keir drawled.

'I'm not,' Darcy said tautly, 'but neither am I an exhibitionist and——'

'You want to retain the nightgown——' a smile flickered over his features '—and display your pearly *décolletage* instead?'

Darcy's mouth compressed. She might have won a battle but he was still armed with plenty of ammunition—ammunition which came from the past.

'I don't see that Anna needs to display anything,' she said brittly. 'She could wear a nightgown with a high neck or perhaps pyjamas.'

In a gesture of frustration Keir ploughed two hands backwards through his hair, rumpling the dark blond strands. 'How about a baggy T-shirt with the Flintstones painted on the front?' he grated. 'Not exactly seduction gear, is it? And,' he added, his tone abruptly softening and taking on a sardonic edge, 'as the one-time wearer of a dress which ought to have been listed under the Explosives and Dangerous Substances Act, you know *all* about that.'

Darcy shot him a murderous look. Why must he continually refer back to her teenage humiliation and how she had acted the vamp? Because it amused him! But how could she have been so naïve and self-deluded? she brooded. Or so brazen?

Her shoulders unconsciously straightened. Such a blunder would not, could not, happen now. Now she had too much savvy and far more poise. Now a man like Keir Robards would never be allowed to play handball with her emotions. A man like Keir Robards— were there any? she wondered. If so she had not met them. Thank goodness.

'Not really,' she said.

He lifted one eyebrow—a brow which calmly and infuriatingly expressed his doubts. 'But to get back to Anna,' Keir continued. 'She's hell-bent on seducing

Marcus, and exposing herself is a come-on, until he reveals he's had the affair with the older woman, at which point she changes her mind. But in the final act he overpowers her and, although she accuses him of using brute force, she damn well likes it and submits and cries—because she's vulnerable!'

Having rammed home his point, he opened his copy of the script. 'Let's go through a couple of the scenes where it's the two of them together.'

They started slowly at first, becoming more fluent as pages were turned. 'You've already learned your lines,' he remarked with satisfaction.

'I thought Jed might not have got around to it, and that it would help if one of us knew what we were doing,' she explained.

'And you have a good Boston accent.'

Darcy grinned, feeling unreasonably pleased and yet at the same time irritated with herself for enjoying his approval. Still, at least she was going some way to vindicating her claims of being a good actress. 'I bought the tape of a book read by a woman who comes from Boston,' she told him, 'and I've been listening to it every day.'

'It's paid off. Now, let's go back and analyse the context of what we've just read.'

Although Darcy had intended to identify other areas where he might disagree with her comments and they could argue again, she did not. Keir centred all his interest on the play and his enthusiasm proved to be so infectious that she found herself working with him, not against him. Besides, most of what he said was valid and irrefutably right.

But as pages were turned she became increasingly aware of his proximity—aware of his denim-clad knee which would rub against hers from time to time, aware of his gesturing hands with the smattering of golden hairs on the backs, aware of the masculine grace of his body.

There was something intrinsically alluring about a *big* man, she mused. And as her awareness of him grew her concentration wavered. She missed lines, fluffed words, lost the general thread.

'Relax,' Keir said, all of a sudden.

'Sorry?' Darcy asked, startled.

'Relax,' he repeated, and, to her great astonishment, he bent his head and kissed her.

As she felt the warmth of his lips an electric pleasure streaked through her. So often as a teenager she had fantasised about Keir kissing her, yet she had not imagined that the blood would swim quite so immediately in her head nor that such an instant heat would invade her body.

Darcy was frantically attempting to overcome her surprise when the question of *why* he was kissing her popped into her mind. Keir had spoken of sexual attraction, so perhaps now that she was older she did appeal? She must. And although it caused a woeful collision in her heart she could not deny that he appealed to her, too.

Darcy had begun tentatively to slide her hands up around his neck and was parting her lips in answer to the drugging pressure of his when Keir drew back.

'No good,' he said.

She looked at him in bewilderment. What was he saying? What did he mean?

'No—no good?' she stammered.

'Anna's desperate with longing even though she's trying to fight it,' he said curtly.

Anna? Who on earth was Anna? Darcy wondered, her thoughts struggling through a mind turned to mush.

Then, a split-second later, it came to her. He had been rehearsing a kiss from the play!

Glancing down at her script, she hastily scanned the lines. Yes, there it was. And you thought he'd kissed you because he fancied you? jeered a cynical voice in her head. What a clown. You didn't turn him on seven years ago, so why should you now? But how could she have overlooked something as potentially nerve-racking as an approaching kiss? Jet lag must be seeping in.

'I'll do better next time,' she told him crisply.

'I should hope so,' he grated.

For a moment Darcy listened to the violent thump-thump-thump of her heart. 'Shall we read on?'

Keir was nodding agreement when he suddenly glanced down at his watch. He swore. 'I didn't realise it was five. No, that'll have to be it for today,' he said, and, rising, he strode over to the desk. 'I'll order you a cab.'

'Er...thanks,' she said, bemused by the abrupt dismissal. A couple of minutes ago the play had been his sole interest, but now he had other, more pressing priorities. What were they? she wondered. Or should it be who? 'You have a date?' she asked as he lifted the telephone.

Keir jabbed out the number. 'Kind of,' he said evasively. 'I'd like you to look more firmly inside Anna's role,' he told her when a cab had been arranged and they had walked back through the house and were waiting outside on the porch. 'And think about her feelings and her motivation.'

'Yes, sir,' Darcy replied, using sassiness to advise him that she was not in the market for changing her mind about the character.

'I mean it,' he said, stern and unamused. 'I'll see you tomorrow, here, at nine a.m. sharp.'

'Yes, sir,' she said again.

Keir's blue eyes met hers in a stormy sideswipe. 'I'd also be obliged if some time during the next few days you could manage to tear yourself away from the splendours of the De Robillard and find somewhere just a little less expensive,' he said as her cab arrived and she set off down the steps. 'You'd be doing both me and the production company a great favour.'

Darcy gritted her teeth. She had been planning to move of her own volition, so it was not necessary for him to tell her. There was no need for him to treat her like some recalcitrant child.

Looking back over her shoulder, she shone a frosty smile. 'Yes, sir. No, sir. Three bags full, sir,' she chanted, and as the anger blazed in his eyes she stalked away.

At the De Robillard Darcy flung all her belongings back into her suitcase and, in less than half an hour, had checked out. She would show Keir that she was no sponger or freeloader, she thought furiously. He would not be given the chance to make one more sarcastic remark.

'Where to?' asked the driver as she clambered into a cab which the top-hatted commissionaire had summoned.

Too late Darcy realised that she should have looked in the phone book or asked for some suggestions at the desk. 'To a less expensive hotel,' she replied.

The driver frowned. He was dark-eyed and swarthy, and looked as if he might have come from an Arabic country.

'Less expensive?' he repeated in a heavily accented voice.

She sighed. He did not understand. 'More reasonable,' she said, but still he frowned. 'Lower priced.' His frown remained. 'Cheap. Very cheap.'

'Ah, very cheap.' The man smiled and pushed into gear. 'Dreamtime Plaza?'

Darcy nodded. Jet lag had fallen over her as suddenly and overwhelmingly as a blanket, and all she wanted to do was find a bed, lie down and go to sleep.

'Sounds good,' she agreed.

CHAPTER FOUR

STANDING at the edge of the kerb, Darcy peered to the right and to the left. She sighed. She had been looking for a cab for almost a quarter of an hour, but without luck. Her gaze fell to the pot-holed road, travelled across dilapidated blocks of low-income housing, along graffiti-scrawled walls. The Washington she had been in yesterday had been clean and smart and cared for, but this neighbourhood resembled a Third World ghetto—and cab drivers might have hesitated to cruise for business here.

She was about to set off again when a shape moved in the corner of her eye. She glanced back. It was a youth with a thin moustache, a close-cropped head and a bandanna; he had been hanging around outside the hotel and had stared at her most intently when she had passed by. He had stopped about thirty yards behind, lighting a cigarette. Or, as he had a skeletal look which she associated with drug addicts, he could have been drawing on something more narcotic.

Darcy felt a twinge of unease. Was he following her or did he simply happen to be going in the same direction? Swapping her script to the other hand, she fitted her bag tight beneath her arm and started walking again, faster this time. A couple of blocks ahead was a crossroads with traffic lights and—please—she would find a cab there.

The Dreamtime Plaza should have been more aptly called the Nightmare Plaza, Darcy reflected as she

61

hurried along. Yesterday evening she had fallen asleep in the cab and, on being awakened at her destination, had gone dazedly through the motions of checking in. Directed to a room, she had undressed, dropped into bed and gone straight to sleep again.

So it had only been this morning when she had realised she was in a dump. The wallpaper was peeling off, the basin in the doorless cubicle which constituted the *en suite* leaked, a film of grime on the windows masked a view of litter-strewn wasteland.

Sneaking a look over her shoulder, Darcy saw that the youth was sauntering behind. He too must have increased his speed for he remained at the same distance. A sense of foreboding crept up her spine. Dressed in a fresh white T-shirt, white jeans and her suede jacket, she looked conspicuously out of place and, with gold studs in her ears and a gold chain around her neck, made a prime target for mugging.

Fixing her eyes on the road junction ahead, she moved into a jog. She felt awesomely vulnerable and horribly lost. Last evening the cab could have gone north, south, east or west and she had no idea where she was.

By the time she reached the intersection Darcy's face was pink and she was sweating. There were no cabs in sight but a look behind revealed that the youth had decided to run, too. With loping strides he was coming closer and he was grinning. She felt sudden, total, crystalline fear. It was a spaced-out kind of grin.

Darcy was frantically wondering whether she should run on, scream at the top of her voice, or hurl her script and hope to stun him, when a ramshackle cab lurched around the corner.

'Stop, stop!' she yelled, waving feverishly and dashing out in front. As the vehicle jerked to a halt she dragged open the door and tumbled inside. 'Georgetown,' she gasped.

The driver turned to scowl. Being forced to brake so violently did not appear to have pleased him.

'Where 'bouts in Georgetown?' he demanded as, on the pavement, the youth raised an obscene finger and sloped away.

Darcy looked at the man in alarm. He had ropes of hennaed dreadlocks with shaved triangles over his ears and a larger one on the crown of his head. While this might be the coolest hairstyle in town, it made him look like a creature from another planet—the kind of creature which leapt out on the unsuspecting from the dark. She shone a wavery smile and quoted Keir's address.

Where were they in relation to Georgetown? she wondered as the cab performed a U-turn and set off again the way it had come. She would have asked, if the driver had not begun to shoot narrow-eyed looks at her in his mirror. Her heart quaked. Could she have escaped one danger only to have landed herself in another?

Ignoring the looks and hoping to spot some identifiable landmark, Darcy peered out of the window. Miles went by, the cab trundled on, their surroundings became more prosperous, but she saw nothing familiar. Anxiety took hold. Had she travelled this far from the city centre last night? Were they really *en route* to Georgetown? Cab drivers came with no guarantee of good character and she could be being transported anywhere, to satisfy all kinds of evil purpose!

On they travelled. Endlessly. Darcy searched for signposts, but the ones she saw bore place names which meant nothing. Don't get paranoid, she ordered herself. This isn't an abduction.

'We're here,' the driver declared all of a sudden.

Darcy frowned out of the window. Where were they? The area was smart enough for Georgetown, yet there had been no remembered roads or shops or houses. Her anxiety was mushrooming when she abruptly recognised that this was Keir's street. They had entered from the other end and must have come into the neighbourhood by a different route from yesterday.

Thrusting the driver the fare he stipulated plus a generous tip, she scrambled out. She was desperate to escape his furtive looks, desperate to be free. Darcy had galloped up to the front door and was ringing the bell when the cab drove off behind her. Thank goodness, thank goodness, a voice babbled in her head.

This morning Keir wore a crisp white short-sleeved shirt, black jeans and trainers. Yet again he looked in excellent masculine shape and yet again her heart performed a loop-the-loop. Darcy frowned. How she could feel such animosity on one level and find the man so desirable on another defied all rational analysis. She had heard of love-hate relationships, she thought drily, and she was beginning to realise what they meant.

After greeting her with somewhat formal courtesy Keir took her through to the study. Sliding his hands into the pockets of his jeans, he surveyed her with cool, cobalt-blue eyes. 'It's almost ten o'clock,' he said.

Darcy looked down at her watch. 'Oh...yes,' she acknowledged in surprise. She had been so distracted by her mugging and kidnap worries that she had forgotten all about the time.

'You overslept?' he enquired, a narrow edge to his smile indicating that while he was prepared to forgive her—just—the lapse had annoyed him.

'No, no, I set my alarm and——'

'You thought you'd do a spot of sightseeing and swing by here as and when,' he stated, his voice cold and clipped. 'Well, although *you* may regard your visit to the States as one long luxury vacation, I don't. As with every member of the cast, I expect you to be prepared to work and I expect you to be punctual.'

Stung by the injustice of his charge, Darcy glared. 'I am prepared to work—morning, noon and night if necessary!' Tossing the script and her bag on to the ottoman, she placed furious hands on her hips.

'As a matter of fact I did go sightseeing,' she snapped. 'I must've spent over an hour being driven around Washington, but there was no tour guide, no taped commentary and no stops to photograph famous monuments. I've no idea where I started off from, though it was a rough and scary area, and no idea where I went on my magical mystery tour. The youth who followed me along the street was pretty scary too, and the cab driver.'

As Darcy recalled her fear the momentum of her anger suddenly stalled and her mouth trembled. 'I thought they were going to—to attack me.'

He frowned. 'What the hell are you talking about? Where have you been?'

'I've come from the hotel——' she shot him a defiant look '—but I've changed hotels.'

'Already?' he protested.

'Yesterday evening,' Darcy announced. 'I was being a good little girl and obeying orders.'

A pulse beat fiercely in his temple. 'Where are you booked into now?' Keir demanded.

'The Dreamtime Plaza.'

'Never heard of the place,' he rasped. 'Where is it?'

'I don't have a clue.' Darcy flashed a saccharine smile. 'But you'll be delighted to know that it's el cheapo. Which explains why my fellow guests resemble what a casting list would term "assorted dead-beats and gangster types" and why many of the people in the neighbourhood seem to fall into the same category.

'It'll also please you to hear that the cashier at the De Robillard was so taken with my English accent that he didn't charge me for my few extravagant hours there,' she continued. 'Though if he had *I* would've paid. Heaven forfend that I should leach away the profits of——'

'Have you been attending a course in bloody-mindedness?' Keir interjected.

'I beg your pardon?'

'In order to take some kind of swing at me, you throw sanity to the winds and deliberately search out somewhere to stay which is in a dangerous area.'

'I didn't——' Darcy started, but got no further.

'You didn't stop and think,' he rasped, his blue eyes glittering. 'That's obvious! Washington is safe if you stick to the tourist haunts in the north-west quadrant, but like all big cities it has its mean streets and there are areas out there where, as they say, it's a jungle. However, if you choose to walk the jungle you can't give me some sob story about being followed and expect my sympathy,' he said chillingly, 'because it's your own damn fault!'

'I don't expect your sympathy,' she shot back, 'but I didn't search out the hotel. A cab driver suggested it and I fell asleep on the way. And if I'd realised the place came straight from the Hades brochure I would never have agreed to go there.'

Keir digested her explanation in silence. 'When did the youth follow you?' he demanded.

'This morning, when I was trying to find a cab. And I wasn't giving you a sob story. He intended to mug me——' Darcy hesitated '—or something.'

'The something being rape?'

She bobbed her head. 'He could've stuck a knife against my ribs and dragged me into an alley and I doubt if anyone would've bothered.' As she remembered how defenceless and at risk she had felt tears trickled at the back of her eyes. She blinked them rapidly away. She was damned if she would cry in front of him. 'He looked like he was high on drugs.'

Keir took a step forward and put his arms around her. 'Honey, you're safe now,' he said softly.

'Honey'? She glanced up at him. The endearment appeared to have slipped out, as much to his surprise as hers, but it sounded fond and caring and made her feel cherished. Darcy laid her head on his shoulder. Keir had broad shoulders and right now she needed someone to lean on.

'The cab driver made me uneasy too,' she went on, compelled to talk it through. 'We drove for miles and miles, and he kept looking at me in his mirror. I know that as a stranger in a strange town I'm more open to fears and maybe my imagination went a little haywire, but——' her voice cracked and tears filled her eyes again '—I started to think that he might be kidnapping me.'

'Don't cry,' he implored, and his arms tightened around her and he started to stroke her back.

'I won't,' she vowed, but his unexpected tenderness proved too much and, as she gazed at him, a single tear brimmed and trickled down her cheek.

'Darcy,' he said in protest, and, raising a hand, he gently wiped the tear away with the tips of his fingers.

'I took a nail-file out of my bag and hid it in the palm of my hand just in case.'

'It wouldn't have been much of a defence,' he said wryly.

'No, but I thought that a sharp jab might just give me chance to make a get-away. I was so frightened,' Darcy said chokily.

'I know and I understand, but it's over,' Keir said, and he lowered his head and kissed her.

Although it began as a soothing, don't-fret kind of kiss, it quickly changed. The pressure of his mouth increased and his lips bit softly at hers as if coaxing a response. And Darcy did respond—she could not help herself.

This time her hands slid up over his shoulders and around the back of his neck, her fingers pushing into the thick dark blond hair which grew at his nape. This time her lips parted beneath his. His tongue—a strong, questing muscle—entered her mouth, and as it moved moistly against hers she strained closer. He tasted faintly of toothpaste and of—himself. It was an intoxicating combination.

As the kiss continued he eased himself slightly away, and as his hand came up between their bodies to cover the high swell of her breast Darcy gave a murmur of delight. Keir ran his fingertips across the peak of her burgeoning nipple again and again.

A shudder ran through her and then, as if in answer to an unspoken request, his fingers were tugging at her nipple, bringing it to a hardness which was a pleasure-pain. Darcy felt a violent spasm between her thighs. She gasped. Her whole body seemed to be a mass of tingling nerves and a need was surging inside her.

Her fingers tightened in the thickness of his hair. Her breathing quickened. Why did she have to be wearing a T-shirt and a bra? she wondered in frustration. Why couldn't she be naked? Being forced to feel the caress of his fingers through the barrier of her clothes when she longed for his touch on the bare pinnacles of her breasts constituted a refined kind of torture.

Keir was kissing her, his mouth searching and biting, erotically devouring hers, when his hand abruptly fell away and he stepped back.

He dragged in a breath. 'That's it,' he said. 'That's the kind of uninhibited passion we need when Anna and Marcus kiss.'

Stricken by a numbing sense of desertion, Darcy stared at him. Keir might not have begun to kiss her as another rehearsal, but some time while their mouths had been fused together he had started to think about the play. Cold fingers squeezed around her heart. She had been lost in a giddy swirl of need while he had been methodically assessing their clinch and appropriating it for Act Three. So much for the power of her feminine appeal! And yet his breathing was laboured so he could not have been entirely immune.

Sweeping back her hair from her shoulders, Darcy shone what was intended to be a careless smile. 'Point noted.'

'I'll take a look at the phone book and see where the Dreamtime Plaza's located,' Keir continued, frowning, and strode over to the shelves behind the desk.

As he started to leaf through the directory she sank down on the ottoman. 'Uninhibited passion'—the phrase pounded in her head. Her passion had been freewheeling, yet she did not usually react that way. Indeed, she could not recall ever becoming aroused by a kiss so swiftly, nor feeling such urgent physical longing—a longing which meant that if the kisses had continued she might have felt compelled to rip off her clothes and offer him her naked breasts, and——

But the kisses had *not* continued. Keir had stopped them. Dead. Darcy's forehead crinkled. Even though his thoughts had been on the play his termination of their embrace had been startlingly abrupt. Why? Could guilt have struck? Had he suddenly recalled his allegiance to another woman—a live-in lover, perhaps? She had toyed with the idea of him living with someone and although she had noticed no evidence of a female touch or female possessions around the house it remained a valid scenario.

Who shared his home? Darcy wondered. Might it be Suzanne Barber? She made a face. Back in the past she had not believed him sufficiently enamoured of the willowy blonde for them to have been having an affair, but she could have been wrong.

As an eighteen-year-old with a rose-tinted view of romance and longing for him to be enamoured of *her*, she could have been guilty of wishful thinking. Probably had. After all, why else would Suzanne, a hot-shot lawyer with a supercilious manner and an acid tongue, have taken special leave from her office—her Washington office, Darcy now remembered—and flown over to see Keir in London, if it had not been to share his bed?

Suzanne could still be sharing it. Jed Horwood might lurch from woman to woman with feckless abandon, but, whatever his other sins, Keir was no philanderer. Or, to be more accurate, neither the theatrical grapevine nor the media had been alerted to a string of affairs, though he was exceedingly adept at keeping his private life sealed off from everyone's gaze.

So might the 'kind of' date which had curtailed their play-reading yesterday have been the need to collect Suzanne at the end of her day's work? she wondered.

Darcy was casting him a speculative glance when it occurred to her that Keir looked uncharacteristically tense and edgy. In kissing him with such abandonment she had unsettled him, she thought wryly... but unsettling him was her aim.

She sat straighter. Cogs whirred in her brain. Maybe she ought to rethink her strategy and take her revenge that way? Perhaps she should embark on deliberate attempts to arouse him and, while the idea was not charitable, give the acid-tongued Suzanne a satisfying dose of comeuppance at the same time?

Her heart jolted into an erratic beat. Such a ploy would demand strong nerves but she had the capacity to look after herself. Didn't she?

'The Dreamtime Plaza is in one of the roughest areas,' Keir said, slotting the directory back on to the shelves. 'However, it's nothing like an hour away so I figure the driver took you a roundabout route in order to bump up his fare.'

'Could be,' she agreed.

'I also figure that he kept looking at you because you're a stunning-looking girl who,' he added pungently, 'like Anna, can be headstrong.'

'Perhaps,' she allowed.

Keir gave a dry smile. 'For sure. Have you thought about your part?' he asked, taking his copy of the script from the desk and coming to sit beside her.

Darcy filed her arousal idea away for further consideration. 'I'm afraid not. I was in bed at around seven last night and slept for a full twelve hours, so there hasn't been a chance. But I'll think about it this evening, cross my heart,' she promised.

'Thanks.'

She slanted him a look from beneath the fringe of her lashes. 'No accusations of idling?' she enquired.

'None. Although you may not believe this I'm actually the most reasonable and charming guy——' he gave a crooked grin '—if the moon's in the right quarter.'

She opened her script. Keir could be charming—and kind and tender and ferociously sexy, that was the trouble. That was what made it so difficult for her to keep it constantly at the front of her mind that he was the enemy. Another difficulty right now was his sitting beside her. Why must she be so terribly aware of the physicality of the man? she wondered in despair.

'How do you see Marcus's character?' Darcy asked, fixing her mind determinedly on work and escaping into the pretend world again.

'As a rough-edged personality with some internal dragons to slay but as someone who, once he's slain them, is capable of deep and unending love.'

'One dragon being his willingness to get involved with the older woman when he and Anna are apart?'

Keir shook his head. 'I don't believe Marcus was willing. I consider that he was drawn into the affair.'

'Against his wishes?' Darcy protested.

'Not quite, but almost.' He leafed through the script. 'See here, where Marcus says...'

They discussed the lines and what each of them thought the playwright had intended to imply, and she had to agree that Keir's version made more sense. An analysis of the theme came next, and although Darcy sometimes found it exasperating to have her views challenged she also found it stimulating to work with someone who had thought so deeply about the decoding of a complicated play and who poured out such energy.

Later they went through another scene, which meant continually stopping to talk about the dialogue and her making many scribbled notes in the margin. Keir, who she discovered had an absolute scorn for playing safe and suggested several provocative ideas, remained dedicated throughout, and keeping pace with him demanded every ounce of her concentration.

'Slapped wrist, Keir,' he said all of a sudden. 'I've forgotten all about lunch and your eyes are glazing over.'

'No, they're not,' Darcy protested, blinking rapidly.

He grinned. 'Yes, they are, and if it's any consolation I'm feeling pie-eyed too. I reckon it's time for a cup of coffee and a sandwich; how about you?'

'Please,' she said, and grinned back. 'I am a bit jaded. When you were working with my father did you forget about lunch then?' Darcy asked as he uncoiled his lean body and rose to his feet.

'I may have done a couple of times, but that's all because, as you know, Rupert was a stickler for his three courses accompanied by a bottle of good wine at one p.m. sharp.' He looked down at her. 'Did I detect a note of disapproval?'

'No, I just wondered.' Darcy hesitated. There was so much she wondered about in the perplexing black hole of their 'differences', so much she needed to know. 'I was also wondering about your being in London on business two weeks back. Does that mean you'll be directing a production there?'

Keir frowned. 'No.'

She waited for more but no more came. In the silence which followed her green eyes darkened. The blunt negative, allied with his failure to so much as hint at what his business might have entailed, irked—and spurred her to make a further enquiry.

'You must've been offered projects in Britain, but you haven't worked there for seven years. Why not?'

At her query, lens covers seemed to drop down over his eyes, shutting off his emotions and shutting her out. 'Because I choose not to,' he said curtly.

'Because of the furore with my father?'

'Furore? I wouldn't call it that.'

'Then what would you call it?' Darcy shot back.

The mood between them had changed. In a matter of seconds they had gone from exchanging grins to verbal warfare.

'Why do you regard me as someone from the Evil Empire?' he demanded.

She straightened out a thumbed corner of her script. In acting dumb he was playing games—but what did she say? The thought raced through her mind that she could fling the root cause of her hostility at him, but that would be like flinging a hand-grenade. The explosion would kill their liaison stone-dead—and consequently maim her hopes of being a success in the play.

Darcy manufactured a smile. 'I don't.'

'You do.' Keir halted, his blue eyes nailing themselves to hers in a weighted pause. 'Though not all of the time.'

The blood burned in her cheeks. She knew that he was referring to her uninhibited response to his kiss, and he knew that she knew. 'That was a mistake,' she declared, striving for her Cleopatra air though not quite making it.

'Some mistake,' Keir drawled. He paused again, frowning this time. 'What did your father tell you?' he asked curiously.

'Nothing.'

His brows soared in stark surprise. 'Nothing?' he repeated, and an emotion which she could not define passed across his eyes.

Was it relief that Rupert had neither complained about nor explained the nature of his tyranny? she wondered. And might Keir now be thinking that he could bluff her into believing that the 'artistic differences' had been of little importance and not his fault? That her father had been the villain of the piece and so deserved to be the victim? If so he could think again!

'Rupert refused to talk about his reasons for terminating your collaboration and withdrawing from the production,' Darcy said tautly.

'Even to you—to Daddy's girl?' Keir protested, as though he could not believe it.

She smiled, cold as ice. 'Even to me. However, he was a dedicated professional who would never have quit unless——'

She broke off. The telephone had given a sudden shrill and when Keir answered it he found that it was the set designer on the line, wanting to talk to him about the scenery.

'Hold on a minute,' Keir requested, and placed his hand over the mouthpiece. 'This may take a while, so do you think you could go and plug in the coffee?'

Darcy nodded. 'And shall I make the sandwiches?' she suggested.

'That'd be great,' he agreed, and swiftly explained where she would find ham and tomatoes et cetera.

In the kitchen Darcy heated the coffee and filled bread rolls. As the call continued she sat down at the table to wait. By saying that he had chosen not to work in Britain Keir had obliquely acknowledged that he had had a compelling reason for staying away, she brooded. And the reason must be that, while he had never demonstrated any sign of regret over his treatment of her father, nor even had the decency to send a few words of condolence when Rupert had died, he had suffered some shame.

I hope it was deep-rooted, sleep-wrecking, corrosive shame, Darcy thought with a spurt of venom. It was only justice that he should suffer.

'I reckon we've done enough work for today,' Keir said when he eventually joined her in the kitchen. 'So suppose I take you for some proper sightseeing?' He grinned. 'You introduced me to the delights of London a long time ago and I'd like to introduce you to Washington.'

Darcy looked at him. Did he genuinely feel that they deserved a break or might he be attempting to sweeten her, perhaps to stem further unwelcome questions about his regime with her father? If she did ask more questions the mood might well become heated again, so settling for a truce seemed the wisest course—at least for today.

'Sounds good,' she agreed.

After they had eaten Keir reversed a well-used, mid-range Ford estate car out of the garage.

'I'd have thought you'd drive something sleek, smooth and sporty,' Darcy remarked as she climbed in beside him. 'Like a Ferrari or a Lamborghini.'

'And become the focus of all eyes? No, thanks. Although I like fast cars I like being incognito even more, which is why I often wear this when I go out,' he said, stretching over to take a dove-grey stetson from the back seat and fit it on to his head. He grinned at her from beneath the brim. 'Anywhere special you'd like to go?'

She thought for a moment. There were so many places that she had mentally marked down to visit in Washington. 'The Smithsonian, please.'

As they drove past imposing memorials and beside cherry trees which were in glorious full bloom Darcy gazed out of the window. But this time her interest in the surroundings was as much to disguise her awareness of the man who sat beside her—the tug of his golden-skinned hands on the wheel, the tensing of his thigh when he pressed down on a pedal, the faint fragrance of his spicy aftershave—as to savour the beauty of the city. Being alone in the confined space of the car with Keir made her feel restless.

'The Smithsonian actually consists of fourteen separate museums which are grouped around the Mall,' he began to tell her. 'There's——'

'Could we go to the National Air and Space?' she requested. 'I read that it's the most visited museum in the world, so it must be good.'

He nodded. 'It is. We'll leave the car here and walk,' he said, swinging the Ford into a parking lot a few minutes later. 'That way you'll get the feel of the openness of the city and the grand dimensions.'

The sky was azure-blue with just a scattering of white cloud. With the tower of the Washington Monument behind them and the splendid bulk of the Capitol building rising in the distance ahead, they strolled along gravel paths which cut between manicured green lawns. Darcy had left her jacket in the car and so, like Keir, was in short sleeves. She started to relax. It was good to feel the warmth of the sun on her bare arms.

'The city is very European,' she said, looking around.

'That's because it was designed by L'Enfant, a French army engineer,' Keir explained, and went on to tell her how the designer had concentrated on Greek classical lines as a reminder to the population of the roots of democracy.

Reaching the museum, they mingled with other visitors who were viewing the array of aircraft which filled the vast galleries. There was everything from monoplanes to manned spacecraft, from the *Spirit of St Louis* in which Lindbergh crossed the Atlantic, to a Pershing missile. They explored the Skylab, and a couple of happy hours later ended their visit by watching a film about flying, which was projected on to a five-storey-high screen and created the illusion of actually being airborne.

'That was fun,' Darcy enthused, smiling as they emerged.

'When I brought my kid brother here a couple of years ago I thought it was fun too,' Keir told her, 'though Steve reckoned touching the moon was more of a thrill.'

Puzzled, she looked at him. 'How do you touch the moon?'

'Like this,' he said, and started shepherding her down the stairs. 'In the seventies the crew of *Apollo 17* retrieved a piece of moon basalt which is around four billion years old and it's available to touch.' When they reached the display he frowned. There was a piece of rock, but it rested behind glass. 'At least it was.'

'Never mind.' He looked disappointed, but Darcy had more interest in his family. 'I wasn't aware that you had a brother.'

'Steve's really my stepbrother. He's coming up to fourteen. I also have two sisters—full sisters. Sadly my father was killed in a skiing accident when he was in his late thirties——'

'How old were you then?' she interrupted.

'Twelve, and my sisters were six and five. My mother was also injured in the accident,' Keir continued, 'and required a series of operations, so the next few years were pretty tough.'

'You had to look after your sisters?'

He nodded. 'I became the head of the family, and as there wasn't too much money around I did whatever jobs I could find in order to help the budget and get myself to college. I pumped gas, waited on in burger bars, worked in factories. It made me grow up fast—perhaps too fast,' he said wryly.

'Which accounts for your inner steel,' she declared.

Keir gave her a quizzical look. '"Inner steel"?'

'You have lots. And eventually your mother re-married?' she prompted.

'Yes, to a guy whose grandfather came from Russia, like hers.'

'Your mother has Russian blood?' Darcy said, in-trigued. 'What about your father?'

'He was of Scottish descent. He and my mother were devoted to each other and for a long time it seemed like she'd never recover from his death. When my mother cares she cares intensely,' Keir explained, and frowned. 'I guess I've inherited something of that. However, several years later she met George and married again. Very happily.' He cast her a glance. 'Has your mother found anyone new?'

'She didn't, and she died eighteen months ago,' Darcy told him.

'I'm sorry.' He touched her arm in an instinctive gesture of sympathy. 'I had no idea.'

'But Mum would never have remarried. Even though Rupert cheated on her, divorced her and had two more wives, she never stopped loving him and always regarded him as a god. A one-man woman who fell for the wrong man,' Darcy observed ruefully. She turned towards the glass doors. 'Thanks for bringing me to the museum today; it's been——'

Keir lowered his head. 'We'll leave in a minute or two,' he muttered, and, taking hold of her elbow, he steered her quickly away from the doors and off to one side of the gallery.

She glanced back over her shoulder. The sudden detour appeared to have been inspired by someone he had seen behind them, and when she looked back she saw a plump, middle-aged redhead in a mauve kaftan, hub-cap earrings and white high heels. Throughout the afternoon occasional looks had come Keir's way—his height and natural grace ensured that—but this woman seemed mesmerised.

'Have you collected a fan?' Darcy enquired.

'Could be,' he said, staring straight ahead as if wishing that he could wrap a magic cloak around himself and become invisible. 'Keep your fingers crossed that she'll lose interest.'

But the next moment there was the noisy clatter of high heels and the redhead ducked around them. 'It's you!' she cried, standing head-on and gazing at Keir like a Venus fly-trap about to devour him. 'It is, it is! Tell me I'm right. Tell me you're Keir Robards.'

For a moment he hesitated, as if tempted to wildly claim some other, very different identity, then he sighed. He circled a glance around and, still holding Darcy's arm, strode behind a large display-board, which removed them from the gaze of the other visitors and forced his fan to follow.

He gave a tense smile. 'I am Keir Robards.'

'I knew it!' the redhead squealed, clapping her hands together with glee. 'I recognised those aristocratic features and——' her voice hushed with admiration '—there's no one who drips class like you do, Keir.'

Although he winced, he bowed his head. 'You're most kind, ma'am.'

'Would you sign a couple of autographs?' the woman pleaded, diving into a large white handbag to produce a notebook and a ballpoint pen. 'First, for me, would you write "to Karon-Anne Moblinski"——' she carefully spelt out the name '—"with love and kisses from Keir"? And then for my daughter...'

The two autographs turned out to be five—no, six—his fan had a neighbour who had been a room-mate at college, she informed him breathlessly, now ran her own hairdressing salon, had two fantastic kids and a weight problem, and went ape over him—but Keir listened to all her gossip, all her instructions and politely obliged.

'It's years since I've seen you on the stage,' she said, finally stuffing her notebook away. 'When are we going to have the joy of seeing you again? I pray that it's soon and in New York. I live in New York.'

'I'll be appearing on Broadway in a couple of months,' Keir told her, and abruptly became the efficient publicist, giving the name of the play, the theatre, performance dates and when tickets would be available. He indicated Darcy. 'And this is Darcy Weston from England; she's playing the female lead.'

The redhead flicked her a glance. 'That right? I'll come and see you,' she assured him with fervour, 'and I'll tell all my friends they must see the show too.'

'Please do. It's been a pleasure meeting you——'

'And for me, Keir,' the woman declared passionately. 'I'll remember it for the rest of my life.'

'—but we must go,' he completed, and, gripping Darcy's elbow, he marched her through the crowds of visitors which were thronging the lobby and out through the doors.

'It's raining,' Darcy said in surprise.

Gun-metal-grey clouds had filled the sky and the rain was knifing down in torrents, which explained why everyone else was waiting inside.

'You want to hang on a while?' Keir asked, casting a wary look behind him.

She grinned. 'And deliver you back into the adoring clutches of Mrs Moblinski? I couldn't be so cruel. Let's make a run for it.'

'OK, but——' he took off his stetson '—you wear this.'

'Thanks,' she said, bundling her hair on to the top of her head and pulling on the hat.

Side by side they set off, sprinting away from the museum building and on to the now deserted paths of the Mall—paths which were awash with water. As they rounded a corner Darcy skidded and almost fell. 'Careful,' Keir said, and took hold of her hand.

On they ran, with the rain spattering their faces and bare arms and making wet patches on their clothes. As they sped through puddles, across flash-flood streams, over springy sodden grass, Darcy felt a spurt of exhilaration. She might have been getting soaked, but to run at full tilt through the rain—with the smell of fresh earth in her nostrils, when they seemed like the only people in the city, with Keir's fingers tightly linking hers—made her feel zingingly alive.

The world was full of promise. Suddenly anything and everything seemed possible. This was how it had been when they had explored London together, she thought, and her exhilaration dwindled away. This was how it had been *before*.

By the time they reached the car and dived inside they were drenched.

'Let me,' Keir instructed as Darcy made to remove his hat. Taking hold of the brim on each side of her head, he carefully lifted the stetson, and the sable-brown curls tumbled silkily down to her shoulders. 'Beautiful,' he murmured.

Her heart cramped. In giving her his hat, then holding her hand, he had made it feel as if they were a couple and now his caressing word had intensified the sensation. But they were *not* a couple. They were not even friends.

'At least my hair is dry,' she remarked, looking at his.

Keir's hair was slicked to his head in a dark gold helmet, with spikes hanging in a dripping line over his eyes.

He swiped back the spikes. 'But the rest of you isn't,' he said as she moved squelchily on the seat. 'You're wet through to your knickers like me.'

'Just about,' she agreed.

Her knickers were white lace bikini briefs, but what kind did he wear? Darcy found herself wondering. Boxer shorts, Y-fronts, a skimpy, sexy black pouch? Or maybe he wasn't wearing any at all?

'And you're cold,' Keir said.

She hastily whipped her thoughts back into order. 'A little,' she admitted. 'How did you know?'

A dimple cut a shadow in his cheek as he smiled. 'Sixth sense,' he said, and his eyes dipped.

Glancing down, Darcy saw that the rain had pasted her T-shirt to her body, making the white cotton almost transparent and, despite her bra, blatantly revealing not only the tight nubs of her nipples but also the dark, shaded circles of her aureoles.

'Trust you to notice—and to comment,' she said, cross with him but also cross with herself because she felt a sexual response. To know she looked so raunchy was arousing her—dammit!

'I'm a red-blooded male,' Keir protested, 'which means I appreciate a good-looking girl with one hell of a body.'

'You are a—a rat fink!' she burst out.

'What does that mean?'

Darcy looked at him. She had heard the expression in an American film, possibly in one of Jed Horwood's, though she had never used it before. 'I don't know,' she had to admit.

'If you're going to insult me at least do it with some degree of articulation,' Keir said, grinning, and his eyes dropped again. 'Ever thought of entering a wet T-shirt competition? You'd be a sure-fire winner. And send a photograph of you looking like that to *Playboy* and their readers would froth at the mouth. Or perhaps *Playboy* have already suggested a photo session?'

Reaching over to the back seat, Darcy snatched up her suede jacket and put it on. 'As a matter of fact another men's magazine did approach me a year or so ago, but I said no,' she told him curtly as she drew up the zip.

'Spoilsport,' he rebuked, and she wasn't sure whether he meant her putting on her jacket or refusing to pose in the nude. He gunned the engine. 'Right, let's go and find the Dreamtime Plaza.'

'You appear to have an aversion to meeting fans,' Darcy observed as they drove out of the parking lot.

Although Keir was concentrating on the rain-lashed street ahead, his interest in her figure—and her own arousal—had disturbed her and she was anxious to change the subject.

'A serious one,' he agreed, and frowned. 'It's the public recognition bit which has turned me off acting, and, while I find directing far more invigorating *per se*, its anonymity is all-attractive. I hate being intercepted by strangers and——' he turned down his mouth '—treated like I'm some kind of pin-up.'

Darcy cast him a sidelong glance. 'You look like a pin-up now. Wet shirt outlining the contours of your manly chest and——' she kept her gaze steady '—jeans clinging to your manly thighs. Send a photograph of you to *Playgirl* and a million women would run amok.'

'Touché,' he said. His face became grave. 'But I don't want to be a fantasy; I want to remain a regular person in people's eyes and maintain a solid connection with the real world.'

'Me too. And as for being recognised—yuck! It makes me go mumbly and look at my feet. Still, it doesn't happen too often, thank heavens. I can still go where I like and do what I want without attracting undue attention.' Darcy grimaced. 'I hate the idea of becoming so well-known that it'd be impossible to visit the local supermarket in peace.'

'But as your career develops you're going to be recognised more and more,' he pointed out.

She heaved a sigh. 'I suppose so, and it's a problem I don't know how I'm going to deal with.' Darcy watched the swish, swish of the windscreen-wipers. 'When you acted you stuck mainly to the stage,' she said, 'and the theatre's my favourite medium. But was that by choice?'

Keir nodded. 'I was once offered a three-year contract by a major film studio, but I turned it down. My agent told me I was insane, but after weighing the pros and cons I decided I'd rather not risk any attendant fame.' He glanced at her. 'If you accept one of those Hollywood scripts that you've been sent——'

'I won't.'

'Does Maurice know that?'

'Yes. The parts are nothing special, though,' she confessed.

'You'd be the bimbo interest?' he asked.

''Fraid so. But Maurice is hoping the play'll bring me such rave reviews that I'll be inundated with top-line film parts that I can't refuse.' She paused. 'Though I will.'

His blue gaze swung to her. 'Your father wouldn't have been pleased,' he remarked.

'No,' Darcy admitted, frowning.

When she had been a baby and her parents had still been married Rupert had appeared in a couple of Hollywood films. Neither had done well, and although he had spent the next six months lounging beside the pool of his rented apartment, waiting for the phone to ring—and making friends with a succession of leggy Californian blondes—no other offers had resulted. He had returned to England, his family and the stage, and consolidated his success there.

Yet no matter how many plaudits he received Rupert had always hankered after cinematic fame and, as she'd grown older, insisted that *she* must win where he had failed. Darcy wiggled her toes in her sodden canvas shoes. If she turned down good roles she would be actively thwarting her father's wishes.

They motored on and in time reached a scruffier area which told her that they must be nearing their destination.

'I'd like to move out of the Dreamtime Plaza today,' she said. 'Can you recommend somewhere else for me to stay?' She darted him a pert look. 'In a respectable area, but modestly priced.'

'I know just the place,' Keir said. 'Check out and I'll drive you straight over.'

'Thanks.'

With leaden skies above and the rain falling the Dreamtime Plaza looked even grimmer and more down at heel. As he drew the Ford to a halt Keir eyed a bunch of youths who were sheltering beneath the corrugated-iron canopy, smoking and chatting.

'Will you be able to manage your case on your own?' he enquired. 'I'm happy to assist, but——'

'I'll be fine,' she assured him, and looked at the youths. 'You wait in the car.'

'Thanks. I reckon it'd be wise—if we're to hang on to the tyres and the steering-wheel.'

After hurrying up to her room, Darcy changed from her wet clothes into a loose emerald-green shirt and white leggings and once again speedily packed.

'I'm checking out,' she informed the bored-looking peroxide-blonde who was sitting behind the reception desk. 'I realise that I may have to pay for two nights——'

'One'll do,' the blonde told her, and cast a disapproving glance around. 'Don't say I said this, but I figure the management should pay you for staying here.'

Darcy grinned. 'I agree.'

As she went out into the rain Keir emerged to take her case and stow it in the back of the car.

'Where is the hotel you're taking me to?' she asked as he thrust into gear and they set off again.

'Georgetown, but I'm not taking you to a hotel, I'm taking you to my house,' Keir told her. 'You're coming to stay with me.'

CHAPTER FIVE

DARCY'S head whipped around and she stared. 'Stay with you?' she echoed.

'That way you'll be kept safe from the mean streets——'

'Thanks, it's a kind thought and I'm grateful, but——'

'—*plus* I'll be able to make sure you turn up for work at the appointed hour,' Keir completed. He threw her a dry look. 'As I recall, the first time we met you arrived way behind schedule.'

'That was unusual and not my fault,' Darcy said indignantly. 'Just as this morning was unusual and not my fault.' She was surprised that he should remember the long-ago evening and her tardy appearance, but she refused to be tagged as a latecomer. 'My normal punctuality rate is ninety-nine per cent.'

'Many congratulations,' he said. 'However, to have you within whistling distance will be so much handier.'

'You make me sound like a dog,' she demurred.

He glanced at her sideways. 'Shouldn't that be a bitch?'

She stuck out her tongue.

'Very adult,' he said.

Darcy considered the idea of moving into his house. Would she be making up a threesome with Keir and a girlfriend—possibly the supercilious Suzanne? she wondered.

'Before you invite me to be a guest, shouldn't you discuss the idea with...someone first?' she suggested tentatively.

'"Someone"?' Keir enquired. 'You mean Cal Warburg? Why? It's got nothing to do with him.'

'No, I mean——' she twitched fretfully at the collar of her emerald-green shirt '—with whoever it is you live with. Frankly, I'm not keen to play gooseberry, and I'm sure that having another woman infiltrate your home-sweet-home is not going to appeal to a girlfriend either. If the roles were reversed it wouldn't appeal to me.'

Abruptly aware of describing a disturbing state of affairs, Darcy gave a lame smile. 'If you live with a girl-friend, that is.'

'I don't.'

'Oh. It just occurred to me that you and Suzanne might've——'

'Suzanne?' Keir said curtly. He frowned out through the windscreen. 'Suzanne's been married for the past six years and, the last I heard, had two small daughters and was living in Illinois.'

And it bothers you, Darcy thought. Why? Did you hope that she might have become your wife and are still pining, still hurt? Earlier, when you spoke about caring intensely, were you thinking of how, despite the passing years, you continue to care for Suzanne?

She gave a mental shrug. The blonde was no longer an issue—for her. But if she had shied away from making up a threesome being one of two was cause for greater concern.

Darcy fiddled with her gold stud earring. Since her father had walked out when she was seven, there had not been a man around the house. Nor had she ever cohabited with anyone. She was not used to a day-today male presence in her life, let alone a continuing close-quarters juxtaposition with a tall, lean-bodied American.

'Nevertheless,' she began, with a somewhat laboured smile, 'staying at your house with you——'

'You don't have a boyfriend who might object,' Keir stated.

'No,' she agreed, and shot him a look, 'but how do you know that?'

'Maurice told me.'

She frowned. She did not appreciate having her love life, or lack of one, discussed behind her back. 'Even so,' she said, starting to protest again, 'I——'

'Darcy, it's staying as in living alongside, not staying as in sleeping in the same bed and conjoining several times a night for white-hot sex,' he drawled.

Her pulses raced. Did he make love several times a night? If he poured as much energy into that aspect of his life as he did into directing, it seemed possible.

'I'm well aware of that,' she said stiffly.

'You're disappointed?' he asked, and she saw a twinkle in his eye.

'Heartbroken,' Darcy declared, defiantly twinkling back, 'but I'll manage in my own small way. However, two months is a long time and we might get on each other's nerves.'

'Don't worry. If you become too unbearable I'll boot you off to a Holiday Inn. I have four bedrooms,' he carried on seamlessly, 'so there's plenty of room. And, when you think about it, what's the point in paying weeks of hotel bills when shacking up with me will——?'

'Cut down on expenses and enable you to wring every last dollar's profit out of the production, thus boosting your personal rake-in,' she finished with tart precision.

He shone a benign smile. 'Every little helps.'

The rain had eased and Darcy looked out at shafts of lemon sunshine which were piercing the dark grey clouds and creating pools of dazzling light on the road ahead. Keir had shown no indication of being a money-grubber in the past, but, as hard cash seemed to have constituted much of the motivation for his directing the play and later agreeing to act, so it was the bottom line in his invitation to stay.

'And I thought the gallant Sir Galahad was worried about my safety!' she said astringently.

She would have preferred to book into a hotel, Darcy thought as they drove along, and yet ... If she was going to alter her game plan and attempt to disrupt Keir's cool with provocative kisses, then living alongside him must present more opportunities, and existing ones were destined to dwindle when the rest of the cast arrived and rehearsals went public.

The gold stud earring was twisted again. Should she equal the score that way? Arguments over the play had to be limited—first, because she was already developing a respect for his opinions and, second, because he would recognise any deliberate contrariness and quickly stamp down on it.

Yet why stop at raising his stress levels? Darcy thought as her internal debate continued. Why not go full out to bewitch and drive him wild and, when the run of the play ended, reject him—ruthlessly, flatly and without mercy? She felt the sting of remembered heartache. As he had rejected her.

She sneaked a look at his profile. Did she possess the power to drive him wild? When she'd been eighteen the answer had been a brutal, ego-flattening *no*. But, as Keir himself had remarked, she had grown up, and in the past two days he had kissed her, caressed her and made appreciative noises about her figure—which were encouraging signs.

And, even if she was not as practised in sexual mores as Keir appeared to believe, the intervening years had taught her a few womanly wiles. Their rehearsing meant that she was lumbered with sessions of physical intimacy, come what may, so why not use them to her advantage? She could attempt to seduce him in their everyday living too. A breath was taken and a decision made. She would seize the chance. Her composure might get a little frayed, but it would not be terminally damaged.

Darcy held on to the seatbelt which crossed her breasts. According to the old adage, what went around came around, and for her to reap her revenge by bewitching him and dumping him would contain a satisfying vice versa symmetry. And then, with the man finally and completely ousted, she would be able to get on with the rest of her life.

When they arrived at the house Keir carried her suitcase up to a bedroom which overlooked the tranquil oasis of the back garden.

'The room's a little smaller than the acreage you occupied at the De Robillard,' he said sardonically, 'but, be it ever so humble, you should be comfortable here.'

Decorated in dusky pink and cream—pink and cream floral bedspread and curtains, cream walls and thick dusky pink carpet—the room had ample wardrobe space, plus its own creamy-tiled bathroom.

'I will be,' Darcy told him. 'It's far cosier than the De Robillard and——' she rolled her eyes '—a vast improvement on the Dreamtime Plaza.'

'While you unpack I'll shower and change,' Keir continued, grimacing as he plucked his still damp shirt from his chest. 'And if you let me know when your case is empty I'll store it in the spare room.'

'Thanks.'

Yet again Darcy unpacked her clothes. She frowned. After being shunted in and out so much, several items were badly creased and needed to be ironed. Two months in a hotel could have been trying, she reflected as she slid a hanger into a crumpled-sleeved blouse. Hotels could be soulless, starchy and restrictive places. But Keir, allowing her free rein in his kitchen as she made sandwiches, indicated that he would be an easy host and not object to her, for instance, using his iron whenever she wanted, or reading his books, or, perhaps, sunbathing in the garden.

When her case was empty Darcy went out on to the landing. She would show that she was an easy guest by putting it away herself, but which spare room did he mean? As they had passed a half-open door at the top of the stairs he had told her that was his bedroom, which left three closed doors—one directly opposite hers and two a little further along. She would try the one opposite.

Curling her fingers around the brass knob, Darcy opened the door and walked inside. Her pulses juddered. Her heart tripped. She had walked into a bathroom where Keir had switched off the shower, stepped out on to a mat and was vigorously rubbing dry his hair. As he rubbed, the fluffy white towel covered his head and fell over his face, and the rest of him was naked—naked and wet-glossed and bronze. When he had been on holiday in India he had collected a dark tan.

Her gaze travelled across the width of his shoulders and well-toned chest. It was surprising how muscular he was without his clothes, she mused, and had a sudden vision of him hurling a javelin in some nude demigod version of the Olympic Games. An arm would rise high above his head and his entire body would stretch, taut with power. He would fling and win. Her eyes moved lower, down over the flat plane of his belly, to his hips and——

'Meets with your approval?' a mellifluous voice enquired.

Her gaze streaked up and, to her horror, Darcy saw that he was watching her look at him. Tufts of half-dry hair made a halo around his head, while the towel was draped over his shoulders, its pristine white contrasting with the bronze of his skin.

Heat flamed her from head to toe. 'I didn't re-realise,' she stammered.

'That I'm shaped like this?' A grin hovered around the edges of his mouth. 'Come now, you must've seen a naked man before.'

Darcy clung on to the case as if it were a lifebuoy keeping her afloat in a choppy sea. 'Lots,' she declared.

'But they weren't so——' his grin spread '—well-endowed?'

She kept her eyes resolutely glued to his face. If only he would cover himself up. Now. Immediately. Please. Keir was teasing her, but was he standing there naked to torment her deliberately? Could be, and yet he was clearly a man at ease with his own body and his sexuality so perhaps he just did not care.

Don't show any reaction, Darcy commanded herself. Don't let him realise that your heart is bouncing up and down like a yo-yo gone berserk. Or that the breath has caught in your lungs. That's what he wants.

'Better,' she declared.

Keir heaved a sigh of mock despair. 'And another illusion bites the dust.'

'What I meant,' she carried on determinedly, 'was that I didn't realise this was a bathroom or that you were inside.'

'So you aren't here to take an investigative peek?'

'No.' Darcy managed a smile. 'I thought you told me your room had its own bathroom.'

'I did and it does, but the shower pump's broken and until it's fixed I'm using the shower in here—the general bathroom,' he explained, and, to her great relief, pulled the towel from his shoulders and knotted it around his waist. He looked down at the case she carried. 'The spare room I meant is the next door along on the right.'

Darcy swivelled. 'Thank you,' she said, and briskly marched out.

Although the next time she saw Keir he was fully dressed, the image of him naked in the bathroom lingered. And throughout the evening, when they had dinner and watched a film on television, it kept reappearing with increasing frequency in her head.

'I'm tired—must still be suffering from jet lag,' Darcy claimed when the clock showed ten o'clock and she could stand it no longer. She faked a yawn. 'I'm off to bed.'

'Sleep well,' Keir said, and wished her goodnight.

She undressed, had a bath and climbed into bed. Switching off the bedside lamp, Darcy lay back on the pillow and closed her eyes. She wanted to sleep, but inevitably a naked, wet and bronzed Keir rose up behind her lids.

When she had slid her fingers inside his shirt at the Brierly she had longed to know how hairy he was, she recalled, and which parts of him the hair covered. Now she did. Now she had seen how a smattering of tawny curls covered his chest, while a much narrower strip of hair speared down over his stomach to his thighs.

Opening her eyes, Darcy stared up at the ceiling. Until she had met Keir Robards she had been blissfully ignorant of the sense-scorching power of desire. She had not known how it could flare and grab hold and dominate. But he had taught her, she thought ruefully, as her mind travelled back over the years...

She had met Keir at her father's house. In order to spend time getting to know the stage crew and organising sound, lighting, costumes et cetera, the young American had come over to London a month or so before rehearsals started and, eager to offer a welcome, Rupert had invited him to dinner. The guests were to have been one of Rupert's co-actors, who was also a lifelong friend, the actor's wife, Keir and the lead actress—a gushing brunette of a certain age.

However, at the last moment the actress had rung to croak that—'Catastrophe, darling!'—she was coming down with flu, and Darcy had been summoned as a stopgap. The summoning phone call had been made when she had been at an after-school tap-dance class, so she had walked in the door, hot, weary and perspiring, and been informed that she was due out to dinner in half an hour.

'I don't want to go,' she protested.

'But I've agreed and you must, to please Daddy,' appealed her mother, who would have agreed to just about anything that Rupert requested.

Although her father's sumptuous Knightsbridge abode was only a couple of miles from the far humbler Cromwell Road flat, there was no way that Darcy could shower, change and be there in thirty minutes. When she did arrive she found her fellow guests marking time in the drawing-room with yet another round of pre-dinner drinks.

'Sorry if I've delayed things,' she said to her second stepmother, a voluptuous, dim, but friendly ex-beauty queen, and stepmother number two hugged her, assured her that she was not to blame, and skittered off to the kitchen to start dishing up the demanding ratatouille *basquaise*, followed by roast wood pigeon and frosted coffee gateau which Rupert had stipulated that she must make.

'You know these folks,' her father said, jovially introducing Darcy to the actor and his wife, 'but you don't know Keir Robards. Keir made his directing début a year ago to unanimous acclaim and he's directing me in my next play.'

Talk about thunderbolts! Forked lightning! And a giant outbreak of goose-pimples! Darcy looked at the man who was rising from the sofa to greet her and recognised Mr Right. By the time he shook her hand she was head over heels in love.

Darcy knew that she smiled far too much that evening, but she could not stop. She also gazed at her dinner partner too much and vastly overdid the hanging on his every word. Keir did not seem to mind. He smiled too, and spent much of his time talking to her.

When he suggested that they share a cab and he would drop her off at home on the way back to his hotel she almost swooned with gratitude. Being alone with him was the answer to all her dreams. It would be *sublime*!

'You know London well,' he observed as they travelled through the lamplit streets and she pointed out famous squares, world-renowned shops and the former homes of historical figures.

'I could show you around if you like, if you have any spare time, if you fancy going for walks, to markets, on the river,' she offered, the words tumbling out over each other. 'We could visit Portobello Road, and Chelsea, and sail down to the Thames Barrier or up to——'

'Any of those would be great,' Keir cut in, laughing.

Over the weeks which followed they met frequently, always at weekends and often in the evenings, and they explored London. While exploring they talked, laughed and established a rapport. To Darcy, loving Keir seemed as natural as breathing, as warm as sunlight, and she knew that although he might not have fallen in love at first sight he liked her. A lot. One heck of a lot. He must, she argued with herself, because he spent so much of his free time with her.

All right, he had yet to kiss her and advance their relationship into the sexual mode, but it was early days and, being an older man with a younger girl, he was rightly chary of rushing things. His discretion was also a kind of courtesy. A sign of respect.

But he would advance things—soon. She could tell from the way his eyes lingered on her mouth and dipped to the curves of her body, from the way he looked at her, pensive and grave, when he thought she did not notice.

Darcy wanted him to kiss her. She wanted them to make love. She wanted it so much that at times she felt dizzy.

Perennially big on gestures and addicted to Saturday-night partying, Rupert invited everyone involved in the production to a get-together at his home. Darcy was there too—officially to help serve drinks, but really because she wanted to spend every last possible moment in Keir's company before he became absorbed in rehearsals, which would start after the weekend. For then, he had told her with a rueful smile, his free time would be minimal.

When Keir arrived she was scurrying back and forth, providing cocktails here, a lager there, and could only manage a snatched greeting, but eventually there was a lull. Looking through the chattering throng, Darcy saw him talking to a slender blonde in her late twenties. She did not recognise her but, with pale hair swept back into a svelte pleat, immaculate make-up and wearing an oyster-coloured grosgrain suit with satin lapels, nipped-in waist and a short, hip-hugging skirt, the woman was ultra-smart. And sexy.

Weaving her way through the crowd, Darcy sidled up beside them. 'Hello,' she said, grinning.

When Keir turned and saw her his brow momentarily creased, making her wonder if, perhaps, she was intruding.

'Hi. This is Darcy,' he told the blonde a little curtly. 'And may I introduce Suzanne Barber? She's——' there was a millisecond's hesitation '—a friend from the States. Suzanne flew in yesterday, unexpectedly.'

His companion offered her a cool hand and a cool smile. They must have come to the party together, Darcy realised. She had not noticed Suzanne with him earlier but, as usual, she had only had eyes for Keir.

'Are you staying in London for long?' she enquired politely, pushing back haphazard wisps of brown hair which, due to her scurrying around, were floating around her face.

The blonde darted a glance at Keir. 'Depends, though anything more than a week'll give my boss a coronary. I'm a lawyer in Washington D.C. and my case-load is heavy right now,' she explained, 'so he didn't exactly jump for joy when I told him I was taking special leave.'

'There was no need to take it,' Keir said.

Slender fingers, tipped with long, rose-lacquered nails, were placed on his arm. 'Sweetheart, it was my choice so you mustn't fret. Our host appears to require your presence,' she went on, indicating Rupert who was waving at him from the far side of the room.

'Could you spare a moment, old chap?' Rupert called, and, after excusing himself, Keir went to join him.

'Keir referred to me as his friend,' Suzanne said. 'That's because we both consider girlfriend to be a rather dated and juvenile concept.' She shone a disdainful smile. 'Though I guess that's what *you'd* call me.'

'Mmm,' Darcy mumbled, aware of being patronised.

Keir had not told her that he had a girlfriend nor ever mentioned Suzanne, though he had said little about his private life. Their talking had been more about her—what she was doing at stage school, for instance—and of the places they visited, of books and films, of here and now.

Darcy stuck her hands into the patch pockets of her ethnic-patterned dungarees. But if he had not bothered to mention Suzanne it followed that she could not be important. Besides, his attitude made it crystal-clear that he liked *her*. A lot.

'I believe you've been acting as Keir's guide to London,' Suzanne continued, in ice-water tones.

As she thought of the fun they had shared Darcy grinned again. 'That's right.'

'He must've found it amusing to have a schoolgirl take him around.'

Her grin faltered. 'Amusing?' she queried.

Aloof grey eyes flicked over Darcy's scrubbed-clean face and tousled hair, then proceeded to make their way wincingly down her dungarees to end at the clumpy black shoes which she wore on bare feet. 'Quite a giggle to be escorted by a teenager who's so obviously gaga over him. But let me put you straight—falling for Keir is a complete waste of your time. His tastes are far more sophisticated,' Suzanne declared, and slid a hand over the sleekness of her hip as if to emphasise her own status as a worldly woman.

'But I'm keeping you from your waitressing and there must be empty glasses to be replenished,' she went on, and waved a hand. 'Off you go.'

Dismissed and feeling insulted, yet not knowing how to protest, Darcy made her way back to the bar table. When she had arrived at the party she had been happy with herself and her appearance, but now she felt like an untidy urchin who was dragging around in clothes salvaged from a shipwreck. She frowned down at her fingers. An urchin with bitten nails.

Did Keir regard her as some kind of infantile comic character? she wondered wretchedly. Was that why he had not kissed her? She had been so certain that she appealed to him, but doubts were beginning to prick like savage pins.

She looked across at Suzanne, who was already deep in a coquettish conversation with the stage manager. The woman might act as if she was God's gift to civilised man and particularly to Keir, but she was not *that* special. Darcy pouted. If she painted her face and wore a come-hither outfit she would look just as smart and adult and sexy.

After school on Monday Darcy took a large chunk of her savings and went shopping. She bought a short white sheath dress. With shoestring straps which tied on the shoulders, a scooped neck and low back, it left little to the imagination and a lot to the eye.

Returning home, she changed into the dress, pain-stakingly made up her face, varnished her unfortunately short nails, sprayed on perfume and, leaving a note for her mother, who was out, went to the Brierly Hotel. In her innocence it never occurred to her that Suzanne might be sharing Keir's room, but it did not matter for when she arrived he was alone. With his jacket shucked off and a drink in his hand, he was relaxing after the first day of rehearsals.

After greeting him and being invited in, Darcy re-moved her coat. She felt nervous and excited. She had come to make it clear that she was not a child, as Suzanne had superciliously insisted, but a woman—a woman who longed to be kissed and who was ready to comply with his secret wish and be made love to. In his room. This evening.

'That's some dress,' Keir remarked.

'You approve?' she asked breathlessly.

'It's different,' he said, his eyes roaming over her. 'You look like a real *femme fatale.*'

Darcy gave a wide smile. So far, so good. This was what she had wanted to hear.

'I've come to ask you if you could give me some help with a character I have to play at school,' she said, quoting the pretext she had chosen.

'Sure. Shoot,' Keir instructed, but then he frowned. 'Your strap's loose.'

As he stepped close Darcy sent up fervent thank-yous to the gods above. The strap must have come loose when she had shed her coat, but it was the perfect accident. It brought them in touch. It possessed the potential to lead to the lovemaking which she craved.

She felt his fingers brush against her shoulder as he undid the strap before tying it up again, and her heart hammered. And when his fingers stopped moving her heart stopped too. As if mesmerised, Keir was gazing down at her breasts in the dipping neckline. For one delicious, thrilling, slightly scary moment she thought he was going to undo the other strap and let the dress slither down to her waist. Then he would marvel at the beauty of her breasts and feel compelled to caress them.

But a split-second later his fingers moved again as he retied the bow. Darcy needed to clench her teeth to stem her frustration.

'Sit down,' Keir instructed, gesturing towards the wing-chairs which stood on either side of the low table.

He went to sit in one and, as he did, Darcy followed and sat down on his knee. She could not sit opposite—she had to be close to him, with him; it was a primal need.

'Darcy,' he said, in a husky protest, 'I don't think this is a very good——'

'There's something I have to say,' she broke in tremulously.

His eyes became sombre and maybe a little cautious. 'About what?' he asked.

'About us,' Darcy said, and stopped, overcome by a sudden shyness. She lowered her head. Keir had taken off his tie and unfastened the top two buttons on his shirt, and as she gazed down she saw curls of dark blond hair in the V. Was all his chest covered in hair? She would know soon. Very soon.

Summoning up her courage, she lifted her head and started again. 'We've had a good time together, haven't we?'

'A great time,' he said.

'Yes.' She slid a finger between two buttons and felt the rasp of hair. Oh, heavens, her skin was tingling and she wanted to touch him all over. 'I—I like you,' she said jerkily.

He looked at her and she felt the air throb. Keir raised a hand and, in what seemed like slow motion, stroked his fingertips across the upper swell of one breast, dipped down into the scented valley, and stroked across the other burgeoning curve. Darcy dared not move. Desire was drumming along her pulses, shrieking in her head, pounding through every part of her body.

'I like you too,' he said.

She gulped in a ragged breath. 'So why are we waiting? I know we've only known each other for a short time and I know I'm young——' she was starting to jabber '—but I'm not that young. Not at all, really. And I'm sure——'

Keir snatched his hand away and stood up, almost tipping her on to the floor. He steadied her, then stepped smartly back. 'I'm not sure,' he said.

'You don't—don't want to?' Darcy faltered, looking up at him with huge, bewildered eyes.

'No. I *can't*,' he rasped. 'I don't know where you got the idea—God knows, it wasn't from me—but——' he gave a curt laugh '—it's ridiculous.'

His words sliced deep into her heart and his laugh made it bleed. She was offering herself to him, offering the most precious gift a woman could give a man, and he thought it was ridiculous? He *couldn't* make love to her? Why not? Did she leave him so cold? Might she even repel him?

As tears blurred her eyes Darcy grabbed her coat and ran to the door. In coming here this evening she had made a monstrous and shaming misjudgement.

'Darcy——' Keir started, but she was already sprinting down the corridor and diving between the closing doors of the lift.

If only she could keep on running to the edge of the earth, she thought as she fled across the lobby—and drop off. If only the reel of time could be halted, reversed and the last half-hour obliterated. If only she had not been so stupid!

Darcy gazed up into the darkness. All those years ago she had not given a thought to Keir's relationship with Suzanne, but now, with cooler and more mature emotions, she saw that it would have been the reason for his rejection. And in comparison with a city-slick lawyer of his own age her teenage *femme fatale* must have seemed absurd.

She punched at the pillow. Even so, he could have let her down more gently; he need not have been so arrogantly dismissive nor so harsh. Yet harshness appeared to be an intrinsic part of his nature, she brooded, for in a different way he had been equally harsh on her father. She drew up the sheet. But her father was dead and she was alive—alive to square the account.

Because he was in the process of learning his lines, Keir suggested that they spend the next couple of days reading through the script, concentrating on the words separate from actions. Darcy was happy to agree. The time in Washington was to be followed by two months in New York—unless, heaven forbid, the play bombed—and she intended to pace her seduction tactics. During rehearsals she would restrict them to their rehearsing; come the previews she would seep them into everyday life and in New York she would come on strong.

For eight hours a day they rehearsed, stopping and starting, and, while she still clung to her interpretation of Anna as tough, each day Darcy was aware of getting a firmer grip on her part. She had never worked with a director who had such a sensitive eye for the texture of ordinary life, and as Keir advised her to 'pinch' some words or 'thicken' others she was aware of him bringing their characters alive.

It seemed odd that she should find working with him so invigorating when her father had found it a disaster, Darcy thought pensively when they were in the living-room, drinking coffee after dinner, on the second day. She frowned at her companion, who was sprawled at the other end of the sofa with his long legs stretched out. What exactly had he done; what could he have said?

'Something the matter?' Keir enquired, noticing her frown.

Darcy sat straighter. He had asked so she would tell him. 'I was wondering about you and my father,' she said. 'He'd never had any trouble with a director before, never had any trouble with anyone in the theatre before, so why did things go wrong with you?'

'No comment,' he said.

'But——'

He stretched forward, putting his coffee-mug on the table. 'If Rupert refused to tell you what happened it's obvious that he preferred that you didn't know.'

Darcy's lips compressed. She could recognise a convenient get-out when she saw one. 'But *I* prefer that I do!' she flared. 'I wish to know what it was that——'

'No comment,' Keir repeated.

'That's it? You're not even going to bother to blame the "differences" on my father?' she jibed.

His brow furrowed. 'That's it. I have to go out to-morrow evening,' he carried on conversationally. 'Will you be OK here on your own?'

Infuriated by his stonewalling, Darcy glowered. She had wanted answers to questions—she *needed* them—but she would not, it seemed, be granted a single one.

'I'll be fine,' she snapped.

'I shall be going out other evenings too,' he went on.

'Please feel free to go out every evening,' she said waspishly. 'I don't care. I shan't miss you.'

Keir looked at her in silence, then stretched up his arms and yawned, revealing a tantalising inch of tanned flesh between the bottom of his sports shirt and the waist of his jeans. 'Y'know, I'm enjoying the acting process again.'

Just as he did not intend to throw any light on the situation with her father, so, by changing the subject, he had indicated that she would be kept in the dark about where he went at nights. Fine; that was his prerogative, she thought caustically.

'What made you decide to become an actor?' Darcy asked stiffly.

As she saw it, she had three choices—she could flounce from the room, or spend the rest of the evening sitting in hostile silence, or follow his cue and talk. She had opted for the third, though only because flouncing or remaining mute seemed childish.

'I didn't,' Keir said. 'I drifted into acting through doing student plays at college and I only took part in them because I had the hots for a girl in the drama group. I was studying economics and intended to make that my career,' he told her. 'However, an agent happened to see one of the college plays and after I graduated he approached me. He insisted I could make it as an actor.

'For a couple of years I held him at bay—I had a job with a finance company which was safe and certain, and I was wary of ditching it for such a chancy profession,' he explained, 'but the guy kept telling me I had talent. I was flattered and acting appeared to offer a world of excitement, so eventually I decided if I didn't give it a spin I might regret it.'

'But after a few years the goldfish-bowl aspect got to you, you did regret, and you packed it in.'

He nodded. 'Though, as a director, I feel that it's been useful to have gone through the experience of acting. With you it was completely different,' he remarked. 'With you it was always taken for granted that you'd go on the stage.'

'I suppose so,' Darcy acknowledged.

'You never wanted to do anything else?'

'Yes, I did. For a long time I wanted to take an arts degree with the idea of becoming a fabric designer—and I still dabble in my own designs—but my mother talked me out of it. She claimed I had acting in my blood and that the stage was my natural habitat. Mum was even keener for me to act than my father, and he was keen,' Darcy said, and fell silent.

She had, she suddenly realised, been programmed from birth to be an actress, regardless of her own inclinations, and the thought troubled her.

'You're getting to know your lines pretty well,' she remarked, in a deliberate change of subject, 'so when are we going to start choreographing the action?'

'In the morning. There's not much furniture in the corner bedroom, so I thought we could arrange it to be as near as possible to the stage for the various acts.' Keir pushed himself upright. 'If we move the furniture now we'll be all set for tomorrow.'

Upstairs, they carried a tallboy and a small cupboard into the other spare room and moved the double bed to a point midway along one wall.

'On stage there'll be a telephone on a bureau there and windows on that wall,' he explained, 'but we can imagine those. And the door is on the left, like now. So, in Act One Marcus walks in and finds Anna sitting at the dressing-table, brushing her hair...

'That was a fancy little performance you put on earlier,' Keir said, switching into character.

Darcy looked at him. A few minutes ago he had been yawning, but now he was alive with energy. She sat down on the stool. She had, after all, said that she was prepared to work morning, noon and night.

'You didn't care for it?' she enquired, in Anna's Boston accent.

He walked over to her and there was the exchange of heated dialogue, during which she leapt up and he grabbed her shoulders, preventing her escape.

'Shall we do the business?' Keir enquired.

Her heart missed a beat. Doing 'the business' meant acting out the kiss which was to follow, but with his impromptu acting he had caught her off guard.

'Um——' she said as the realisation that this was the time to start her seduction tactics clamoured in her head.

'We are supposed to be physically easy with each other,' he said. 'We are supposed to be lovers.'

Darcy gulped. 'Um—yes.'

'So some practising wouldn't go amiss.'

'Um—no,' she acknowledged.

Changing back into Anna, she pushed at him, they struggled, and he gave her a punishing kiss. It began as the mouth-on-mouth 'chewing' which was used in the theatre to simulate kissing, until Darcy parted her lips. Then it became a real kiss. A deep kiss. A long kiss.

When it ended Keir drew back to frown. Her heart pounded. Was he going to ask what she had been doing and accuse her of breaking the rules? Was he going to say it must not happen again?

'Enough passion?' she enquired.

Her gaze was rock-steady and her voice cool; it was the finest acting she had ever done.

Keir gave a curt nod. 'Now let's move to Act Three and the tying scene.'

'Whatever you wish,' she said, and, walking past him, she lay down on the bed.

Throughout another fiery exchange of dialogue Keir sat over her, then he caught hold of her wrists and drew them above her head towards the rails of the bed.

'And Marcus reaches out for a scarf she's left on the bedside table and ties her up,' he said. 'Then, after telling her he loves her, he lies down alongside and kisses her.'

Darcy looked up at him. He was leaning over her, still holding her wrists. She snatched in a short, quick breath. He had said that his Neanderthal behaviour might give her a thrill—and it did. Her nerve-ends were electric. Her mouth had gone dry. Could his Russian blood be that of a Tartar? There seemed an air of the wild, rampaging horseman about him.

She frowned. She felt restless and lusty, and full of a crazy desire to reach up and kiss his lips.

'In my humble opinion I think Anna should break free,' she said.

'But Marcus still kisses her?' he demanded impatiently.

'Oh, yes, he must because——'

'Damn right he must,' Keir growled, and his mouth covered hers.

This time there was no simulation; this time the kiss was for real from the start. His tongue thrust between her lips and entered the moist confines of her mouth, a sensual invader. He let go of her wrists and, as the kiss continued, lowered himself down on the bed beside her. He clasped her waist, but in time his hands moved down to take hold of her hips, pulling her against him.

Darcy's head began to spin. She felt drugged by the closeness of him, the heat coming from his body, his clean male scent. Her breasts were swelling, her nipples distending, and there was a quicksilver ache between her thighs. She strained closer and as she felt the hard shaft of his manhood a storm of passion seemed to break inside her and she gasped.

'Is that going to happen on stage?' he murmured.

Darcy drew back, separating her hips from the thrust of him. What were they doing? she wondered dazedly. Everything was going too fast and too far, cannoning out of control.

'Sorry?' she asked.

'Are you planning on having an orgasm?'

She looked at him, her eyes wide and shocked. 'An—an orgasm?' she sputtered.

'You didn't think I'd realised?' Keir drawled.

Darcy gulped. Her composure was not merely frayed right now, it was unravelling at a rate of knots. But she would give as good as she had got.

'How about you?' she enquired, glancing pertly down and adopting a playful tone as her first requisite. 'Will that happen on stage?'

'In front of eight hundred people?' he said drily. 'I doubt it. However,' he went on, 'I guess I'd better take a cold shower.'

Darcy leapt up from the bed. 'Then I'll say good-night,' she rattled off, and sped out through the door.

From that evening they seemed to enter into an un-spoken agreement whereby, as if knowing that rehearsed kisses would inevitably become the real thing, they abandoned all pretence and kissed properly. However, Darcy took care to keep a small part of herself aloof, to control her responses and not become so carried away again. The trick was always to remember that she was making Keir *pay*, she told herself. And it worked. Just.

Yet although they kissed almost every day she did not feel at physical ease with him. Just the opposite. She was always agonisingly *aware* of him as a desirable sexual animal, and of the dangerous game which she was playing.

But she was learning to know his body. She knew the exact moment when, momentarily, his desire for her took precedence over his acting. It was a subtle shift, yet a shift all the same. His grasp on her tightened, his breathing quickened and, on occasion, his body would start to become acquisitive.

It excited her. And as the days went by Darcy found it harder and harder to retain her aloofness. Now the evenings when Keir disappeared to wherever he went were useful. They provided a much needed break from his presence and gave her time to regain her poise.

'The rest of the cast are arriving today, and tomorrow rehearsals start at a community theatre,' he told her one evening. 'We'll be there until we move into the proper theatre, three days before the play opens.'

'I'm looking forward to meeting everyone,' Darcy replied.

She spoke the truth. Having other people around would force the situation between them to cool down for a while—which would be a relief.

CHAPTER SIX

'DOWN, two, three, up, two, three,' the voice in the ear-phones of Darcy's personal stereo instructed. 'Now, hands at your waist and lift those knees. Lift them high.'

Alone in the women's dressing-room and stripped down to a white lace wisp of a bra and bikini briefs, she went through her exercise routine. It was lunchtime and, instead of accompanying the rest of the cast to a nearby local diner, today she had chosen to stay behind at the theatre, eat an apple and work out. If she was to appear semi-nude in public she needed to keep well-toned and in shape.

Her brow furrowed. Whether she would appear semi-nude had yet to be settled. She and Keir had acted out the scene fully dressed, but she had still to try it naked beneath the sheet, which was when the decision would be made. Darcy jogged on the spot. Like the tying scene, which, after repeated wrangling, they had agreed would be left 'to mature', it needed to be decided soon.

As she kept time with the music Darcy's thoughts meandered on, first to how extraordinarily good Keir was in his role and then to her fellow actors. They were a pleasant bunch. There was Thea Crosby, a bubbly, auburn-haired woman in her mid-forties who played the older female, and Saul Swift, a curly-headed Adonis with a boyish smile who played the character with whom Anna had had an affair, plus two middle-aged actors and one elderly actress who filled lesser roles.

She had never met any of them before and yet, after just a week, they had become a team. Much of this was due to Keir, who inspired a deep sense of mutual purpose which had drawn everyone together. At rehearsals there was commitment, laughter, occasional raised voices, for people did not always see eye to eye, and much diligence. And at rehearsals Keir had skipped over their clinches and kisses.

'Darcy and I have things organised so there's no need to go through it all again right now,' he had decreed.

Common sense said that she ought to be grateful for this respite and yet, even though their acted-out intimacy would have taken place beneath the gaze of others, increasingly she found herself feeling...deprived. It was as though kissing Keir were a drug to which she had become addicted and she was suffering withdrawal symptoms. Darcy bent and stretched. Her reaction was unexpected, curious—and unsettling.

She switched her mind back to the general camaraderie and how Keir worked with the cast as a team. According to one of the middle-aged actors who had been in a couple of his productions, that was how he operated—which made his clash with her father even more of an enigma.

Darcy was theorising that Keir might have singled out Rupert for his dislike because he had resembled a person who had done the dirty on him in the past—which admittedly did not seem much of a theory, more a rather wild surmise—when she had the creepy sensation of someone watching her. She shot a glance over her shoulder. Saul Swift was lolling against the closed door with his arms folded. She frowned. He looked as if he had been there for quite some time.

Abandoning her exercises, she switched off the tape. 'You're...back...early,' she panted.

'I returned ahead of the others—to see you.' Saul shone a smile which ranked as a borderline leer. 'And I did.'

Uneasily aware of the skimpiness of her underwear and how his eyes were glued to the compulsive rise and fall of her breasts, Darcy reached for the floral, button-through dress which she had been wearing. 'You wanted something?' she enquired.

The young man stood up straight. 'You,' he said.

She pulled on her dress and started quickly fastening the buttons. From the start Saul's friendliness had contained an element of sexual interest which, because he was newly married, she had told herself must just be his manner and so had ignored. But she could not ignore his returning alone to the empty building, sneaking into the dressing-room and violating her privacy. She could not ignore his making a pass.

'I'm not available and neither are you,' Darcy said, smiling to show that she had no wish to offend him.

'Not available? You mean you and Keir are——' on the point of crudely describing the activity that he imagined, Saul substituted a more discreet word '—involved?' His lip twisted. 'I should've have guessed as much.'

'We're not involved,' she said, 'but you do have a wife.'

'And an open marriage,' came the glib reply. Smiling his boyish smile, the young man stepped closer and slid an arm around her waist. 'Loosen up, babe,' he exhorted.

She unwound his arm. 'Open marriage or not, I do not mess around with married men,' she said crisply.

'There's always a first time,' he replied.

'Not for me.'

'Miss Prim and Proper, are we? I can't believe that.' His gaze smeared over her. 'You have a body built for sin.'

'And you talk like someone in a B movie.' Stepping past him, Darcy opened the door. 'Out,' she instructed, and, because she did not want any bad feelings, she added, 'Please.'

Saul did not move. He was a handsome young man and women did not often rebuff his advances. On the contrary, they usually threw themselves at him.

'You'll change your mind,' he said.

'I won't.'

'Soon,' he told her smugly.

'Never. Hi, Thea.' Darcy grinned thankfully at the actress who was approaching along the corridor. 'Bye, Saul,' she said, pointedly waving her fingers. The actor scowled and walked away.

'The Press, in the shape of one Herbie Krantz, gossip columnist and Nosey Parker, pounced on us when we were in the middle of lunch,' Thea said as she came into the room. Dressed in a symphony of beiges, walking on perilously high heels, and with her eyes dramatically painted, she was a glamorous figure. 'He wanted to ask questions there and then, but Keir held him off and he's coming here later this afternoon. Beware; Herbie's a sleazeball who thrives on scandal.'

Darcy smiled. 'Thanks. I'll remember that.'

Sitting down, Thea took a slim silver case from her handbag, extracted a cigarette and lit it. 'Herbie can be a bolshie so-and-so, but Keir handled him beautifully.' She blew a perfect smoke ring. 'As you'd expect. Of course, it's because Keir handles everything so well that Cal Warburg's given him complete freedom with the production. Cal knows that whatever he decides it'll be right.'

'Mmm,' Darcy said, and started to comb her hair.

As the days had passed it had become clear that Thea not only admired Keir's directing skills but fancied him too. In his company she became that extra bit vivacious. She also sat close to him whenever she could and, Darcy had noticed, touched him. It was just a casual hand on his shoulder here and a stroke of his arm there, but a touch—a *caress*—all the same.

Being at least seven years his senior clearly did not worry her. Nor did it worry Keir, for his attitude towards the actress was calmly appreciative of both her talent and her beauty. Darcy frowned at her reflection in the mirror. Maybe it was irrational, but the woman's touching him, and his acceptance, rattled her—especially now that *their* touching had ceased.

To Darcy's relief, when the rehearsals resumed Saul appeared to have forgotten about being turned down and was amiable again. They read a scene together, and read it well. The run-through continued and with amazing speed the afternoon disappeared. Keir was making wind-up comments when a diminutive, sharp-featured man in a black polo-neck, white chinos, and carrying a tape recorder, swept down the centre aisle.

'You agreed I could have a chat,' he called to Keir as he ran up the steps on to the stage, and Darcy realised that this must be Herbie Krantz.

Keir nodded. He gave him general facts about the production, followed by a précis of the play. Next he introduced the cast, who provided potted career histories.

'That suit?' he asked, when everyone had taken their turn.

The reporter hesitated, as though he had hoped to embark on more personal questions, but then, apparently deciding these would be vetoed by Keir, he nodded. 'Thanks,' he said.

As the gathering broke up and people started to leave Saul strolled over to the gossip columnist. 'Thought you might be interested to hear that Darcy's moved in with our director,' he said in a low voice. 'She's been living in his house for three weeks already.'

Just within earshot, Darcy froze. Far from accepting her dismissal, the young man was retaliating with this spiteful off-the-record announcement. And Herbie Krantz's beetle-black eyes were shiny with interest.

She went up to them. 'I'm living in Keir's house as a work colleague,' she said, frowning at Saul, who did not seem in the least bothered that she had overheard. 'And with my own bedroom.'

'Her own room, but,' the actor said, with a suggestive smirk, 'alone together through the long dark nights.'

She looked over to Keir for help, but he was talking to Thea.

'It's a working arrangement,' she insisted, 'and no big deal.'

'You guys aren't having a fling?' asked the reporter.

'We are not,' she said firmly.

'"The lady doth protest too much, methinks,"' chanted Saul.

Her eyes shot green sparks. 'And methinks you are one big troublemaker!'

'Ready, Darcy?' Keir called, from the side of the stage.

'He's taking her back to the love-nest,' Saul informed Herbie Krantz, *sotto voce*.

Darcy clenched her fists. 'There is no love-nest,' she said, grinding out the words as if she were grinding them on metal.

'I know that, doll,' said the gossip columnist, but he winked broadly at Saul.

Fuming, she joined Keir and went with him to the car. 'Saul has given Herbie Krantz the idea that we're lovers,' she said as they swung out on to the road, and furiously relayed the conversation.

When she had finished Keir shrugged. 'Never mind.'

'Not mind?' Darcy protested, turning to frown. 'You mean you don't?'

'Most times I would, but if Herbie drops a hint or two of a romance in his column, and it seems as if he's bound to—well, it could be good for the play.'

She stared at him. She did not believe what she was hearing. 'But other newspapers might pick up the story and——'

'If we're thought to be lovers it could whet the public's interest and make more people come and see us. And we need an audience.'

'So anything goes so long as it boosts box-office receipts and helps the production?' she demanded.

'More or less.'

Darcy eyed him with as much icy disdain as she could muster. 'Great attitude!' she snapped, and sat in angry silence for the remainder of the journey.

'It's high time we settled on how we're going to play the tying episode,' Keir said as he parked on the drive. 'We must also go through the sheet-wearing scene. We need to see how it goes and what you feel about it.'

Darcy forgot about Saul's troublemaking and Herbie Krantz. The sheet scene had been nagging at the back of her mind and the more she thought about appearing topless in public, albeit for a brief moment, the more uncomfortable she felt.

Other actresses might strip off at the drop of a hat, and justify it by claiming that they were doing so for the sake of the plot and in the furtherance of dramatic art, but she was a private person and the prospect of being ogled by every Tom, Dick and Harry did not appeal. Besides, in reality, nudity was often used to jig up flat productions, she reflected as she climbed from the car, but this one needed no jigging.

'I'm going out after dinner tonight, though only for a couple of hours,' Keir continued, 'so when I come back——'

'Let's do the sheet scene now, right now,' she said, suddenly desperate for the matter to be decided—one way or another.

He looked at her over the roof of the car and shrugged. 'OK.'

Darcy changed into her nightgown—a filmy cream silk chiffon affair which, although it came up to her throat at the front and tied at the nape of her neck, plunged to her waist at the back—and joined Keir in the corner bedroom. The bed was already made up and she climbed hastily between the sheets.

Earlier, she had been aware of being in a state of undress before Saul and now she was aware of being undressed in front of Keir, though her feelings were different. With Saul she had felt ill at ease and threatened, whereas now an excitement tingled deep inside her.

'We'll do the dialogue,' Keir said, 'and you go through the actions.'

At the appropriate moment Darcy drew the nightgown off beneath the bedclothes and tossed it aside. Loosening the sheet, she wrapped it under her arms, sat up and tied it in a knot between her shoulder blades. She rose from the bed. Her heart thumped. The prospect of appearing topless before the general public worried her, yet to reveal her breasts in private before Keir seemed a million times more nerve-racking.

'Hold on a minute,' Darcy said. The sheet was double-size and yards of white cotton were drifting around her. She gathered up a bunch and tucked it into the knot. Speaking her lines, she advanced on him. Her fingers curled around the top edge of the sheet, Darcy took a breath—and lowered the material. The knot broke. The entire sheet fell. 'Damn!' she said, grabbing feverishly at the loose material which was wafting from behind and gathering at her hips.

Keir chuckled. 'Need any help?' he asked.

As he stretched out an arm she leapt back. 'No!' she yelped, plucking and hoisting. Her bare-breasted exposure had been intended to last for one second, but it seemed like hours before she managed to cover herself up again. And Keir's watching on in amusement did not help.

'It won't work,' she declared, hot-faced and flustered. 'If the sheet collapsed like that on stage——'

'People would talk about it, the media would pick up on it and we'd have queues of guys three deep at the box office,' he said with a grin. 'All praying that on the night they see the play you'll have trouble with it again.'

Darcy flashed a brittle smile. 'And, hey, anything goes so long as it helps the production.'

'You said it. Let's start again from scratch,' Keir instructed, becoming businesslike, 'and this time see if you can't roll the sheet around you.'

'But there's so much of it that I'll end up looking like an Egyptian mummy,' she protested, frowning at him as she stepped backwards to the bed. 'And—— Oops!'

Her foot had caught in a fold of cotton which was trailing on the floor, trapping her. Darcy kicked for freedom, managed to hobble her other foot in the attempt, and, with both feet effectively manacled, started to overbalance.

'Careful,' Keir said, striding forward.

She felt herself falling, grabbed wildly for his shoulders, and, in a flurry of loosening sheet, pulled him down with her as she toppled back on to the bed. Winded, Darcy lay there trying to catch her breath, then her heart began to pump. It was a week since they had had any physical contact, but now Keir was sprawled half on top of her, and the feel of his body, his weight, had a disturbing effect.

'Sorry,' she said, frantically squirming out from under him, though they still lay alongside each other.

'Were you born to tease?' he demanded.

Darcy looked at the tanned face which was only inches from hers. He seemed impatient and annoyed—bereft of his usual cool.

'I beg your pardon?'

'Seven years ago you visited me at my hotel wearing a please-touch-me dress and when I duly obliged you proceeded to exit. These past weeks you've been kissing me in a remarkably energetic way, but have restricted it to our rehearsals.' He turned his head and his cobalt-blue eyes travelled down her body. 'And now...'

Not knowing what 'now' meant, Darcy flicked a parallel look downwards. Her cheeks flamed. When they had fallen the sheet must have opened and twisted beneath them, for now, while a slender wing of white cotton lay decorously across her thighs—thank goodness!—the rest of her was naked.

'You can't believe I meant this to happen on purpose?' she protested, snatching sideways at a piece of sheet which, because it turned out to be just a few spare inches, made a totally inadequate covering.

'What I believe,' Keir said, his tone curt, 'is that you're playing fast and loose with me.'

Darcy's mind raced. The accusation was correct, but did he also mean that he considered *her* to be fast and loose? If so he was wrong. Laughably wrong. Her fingers clutched tight at the spare edging. She objected to his error, though, as she was lying with less than half of one breast covered, like a stripper approaching the finale of a risqué horizontal striptease, it did appear to have credibility.

Desperate to cover herself up, Darcy looked around and spotted her nightgown on the floor. Set on retrieval, she was pushing herself up on her elbows when a firm-muscled arm shot out, preventing her escape and bolting her down on the bed.

'I want to get my nightgown,' she protested, snappy in her agitation.

'And you shall, if you ask nicely...' Keir paused, his eyes lowering again and his voice taking on a purring quality '...but only when I've finished looking at you.'

'You bastard!'

'That wasn't what I had in mind.'

Darcy pushed fiercely at the arm which lay across her waist, but he held her in a grip of iron. 'Let me go!' she demanded.

She pushed again, and wriggled and squirmed—until she became aware of his interest in the sway of her breasts. She also realised that in wriggling her midriff against his arm, skin on skin, she was in danger of exciting herself. Her wriggles ceased and she lay rigid, like a flush-faced and tumble-haired statue.

'There's no need to stop,' Keir drawled.

Her look shot daggers. 'I shall wear a nightgown on stage,' she declared through gritted teeth.

'What?' As he gazed down at her slender body with its high curves his blue eyes seemed to smoulder.

'I shall wear a nightgown,' Darcy repeated, ready to do battle and determined to insist. 'You may be the director and keep Cal Warburg tucked in your back pocket, but I have rights too!' She glanced at the frothy puddle of cream chiffon which lay so near and yet so far away. 'I shall wear that one.'

'Sure, sure,' he muttered. 'The sheet's far too unwieldy.'

'You agree?' she asked in blank surprise.

'Yeah.' Keir raised his hand towards her mouth, a long index finger extended. 'Suck it,' he said.

Bemused by the so-easy victory, Darcy opened her mouth and sucked. Her nerves jolted. To have his finger between her lips and to be licking his skin, wetting it, tasting it, seemed alarmingly erotic. Her tongue glided over the smoothness of his nail, his knuckle, a roughness of hair. What was he doing? What was this *for*? As he withdrew his finger she started to ask, but her words faded on the air.

Keir had touched his fingertip to her breast and was circling it slowly around the base of her nipple. Sensation streaked, as fast and slicing as a laser beam, from her breast to the cluster of nerves between her thighs. As she felt the petalled flesh leap and pulse she bit hard into her lip, steeling herself against showing any outward reaction. He lifted his finger across the burgeoning peak, moistening the wine-dark skin and rhythmically caressing it.

She inhaled a swift breath. He was no longer pinning her to the bed and she could have risen, but a languor was invading her limbs. A dizzy sloth had filled her head. What he was doing might be sensual torture, yet she did not want to escape.

'Again,' Keir commanded, raising his finger to her mouth.

Darcy obediently licked again. This time he moistened her other nipple, massaging and gently rubbing the zinging flesh until her body arched beneath his touch.

'Keir,' she murmured in helpless protest.

He looked down at her with grave blue eyes. 'Did you think you could deliberately arouse me and stop, time after time, and I'd go along with it for evermore?' he said thickly. 'It doesn't work like that. I'm not made of stone. I'm a man with a man's impulses and a man's needs, and I want more.'

Darcy's heartbeat quickened. 'More?' she asked unsteadily.

'You're a beautiful young woman with a body made of silk and——' he drew a slow finger down between her breasts, over her midriff and to the hollow of her navel '—you're driving me out of my mind.'

She shone a tremulous smile. Although the pacing of her seduction tactics seemed to have gone drastically awry, they were working and so they must be continued, despite the disturbing personal penalty being imposed.

Remember that every time he touches you—the way he's touching now—you're reaping your revenge, said a distant, almost forgotten voice inside her head. Try. Try harder.

'I am?' Darcy said huskily, and stretched, lifting her body towards him.

He took a rough breath. 'Wanting to look at your breasts, to touch them, has been driving me crazy. *You're* driving me—— Hell!' he rasped, abruptly raising his head.

'What's the matter?' she asked, but as she spoke she heard the doorbell ring. 'Ignore it,' she said.

'Shall I?' For once in his life Keir seemed uncertain.

She placed a hand on his shoulder. She did not want him to go. He had to stay with her. And touch.

'Yes.'

He was silent, as if torn, but as the bell rang again he rolled from her and levered himself up from the bed. 'I'd better answer it. Whoever it is will've seen the car, so they know someone's at home. But in any case,' he continued, heading for the door, 'I'm due out in an hour and we've still to eat.'

As he disappeared Darcy shut her eyes. She had been deserted and why? Because some interfering idiot was ringing the bell and because Keir felt hungry! Taut with frustration, she swept up from the bed, grabbed her nightgown and marched back to her own room.

As the murmur of conversation sounded at the front door she flung on her clothes. She brushed ferociously at her hair. She resented his abandoning her with such speed and she resented his going out this evening. She had said she didn't care when he disappeared on his mysterious excursions, but she cared. Greatly. Where did he go? What did he do? For all she knew he could be meeting a woman—maybe even Thea.

When she heard the front door close Darcy stalked downstairs. She found Keir in the kitchen, cracking eggs into a bowl.

'I thought we'd have an omelette; it's quick and easy,' he said.

She gave a brief nod and started to set the table. Although a woman came in to clean and attend to the laundry twice a week there were meals to be made and, with surprising ease, they had developed a routine whereby they would decide on menus, shop for food together, and subsequently share the preparation.

Because she had once taken a cookery course when she had been between jobs, Darcy tended to make dishes like sweet and sour pork or chicken in a pastry case, while Keir did simpler things. He did them well, and willingly.

'That was Herbie Krantz at the door,' he told her as he whisked the eggs. 'He said he needed to check a few details about the play, but I reckon he came in the hope of checking out our romance.' His lips stretched into a wry smile. 'All it would've needed was for you to have appeared at the top of the stairs, dressed in the sheet— or not dressed in it,' he added, with the significant arch of a brow, 'and——'

'You'd have confessed that there was a romance and said you'd sell the story—for a price?' Darcy interrupted. 'Or have you already sold it to him? Or perhaps you've decided to wait until more journalists latch on and then you can auction it off to the highest bidder? After all, you do appear to be motivated by that motto from the 1980s movie *Wall Street* which said "Greed is good".'

There was a flash of anger in his eyes. 'You have the wrong idea about me,' he rapped.

'Do I? You want to make as much money as you can from the play, so why not make the money that way too?' Darcy knew that she was being nasty, but her frustration meant that she needed to attack him somehow. 'It may be a little unsavoury, but so what? It's the dollars and cents that count.'

'I don't want to make money for myself,' Keir said brusquely. 'I want to make it for a charitable trust.'

She positioned the water glasses, one for him and one for her. 'A trust?' she queried.

'It was established a few years back to provide business know-how for young entrepreneurs all over the world, with an emphasis on those from poorer countries,' he said, oiling the pan and placing it on the heat. 'Although there's a good deal of help which can be given funds are limited, but after much arm-twisting Cal Warburg agreed that whatever profit percentage I make he'll give the trust an equal donation.'

He poured the egg mixture into the pan. 'Cal upped the ante when I agreed to act, but that's why I'm eager for us to make as much as we can.'

Darcy felt small. And ashamed. 'How did you become involved with the trust?' she asked.

As he cooked the omelette, and later over dinner, Keir explained how a fellow economist with whom he had once worked had appealed for his help in making a promotional video for the trust. He had agreed and, on learning more of its aims, had suggested that video-based business skills tutorials could be useful.

Delighted with the idea, the trust's board had asked if he would organise a series of videos which would need to be slanted towards the differing needs of different countries. Although this was an intensive, long-term undertaking which would have to be fitted around his working life, he had agreed again. And this had led to his spending time abroad as he researched specific requirements and filmed locally.

'That's why you went to India?' Darcy enquired.

'Yes, and I was in London to liaise with the guys who run the British end of things.' Keir frowned. 'I guess I should've told you about this before, but I dread the Press finding out and so I've made it a rule never to talk about it.'

'You don't want to be portrayed as a do-gooder?'

'Hell, no! And I'm not. OK, I made the videos for free, but doing them has taken me away from the neuroses of the entertainment world and introduced me to all kinds of interesting people.

'It also gave me the idea for setting up my own business videos company,' he carried on, 'and from the discussions I've had with various commercial organisations it's clear that there's a huge market for that kind of thing.'

'You're not going to give up directing plays and films?' Darcy protested. 'Keir, you can't!'

He smiled at her plea. 'No, but from now on I intend to make videos in between directing assignments. With luck, they'll provide a decent income and mean I'll never be forced into taking on jobs that I don't like. I was in the middle of completing the editing of the trust's videos, before launching my own company, when Cal approached me about the play. Which delayed things and forced me to work on them in the evenings.'

'That's what you've been doing when you've gone out?'

He nodded. 'But no more, because the last one'll be finished tonight, thank goodness.'

'So whenever you disappeared between directing jobs you were busy with the videos?' Darcy questioned.

'No, just for the past two or three years. Before that, if all I was offered was second-rate stuff, I studied—and hoped like crazy that something decent would turn up.'

'Studied?' she asked.

'My directing career might seem like one long stroll down Easy Street,' Keir said wryly, 'but I've put in a hell of a lot of time watching people, their mannerisms, their reactions. And because I never had any formal training I've also made it my business to learn as much as I can about lighting, sound, camera angles—all the practicalities which go into a stage or film production.'

Darcy considered this. 'And you refuse assignments if they don't appeal?'

'Yes. Despite having had what the papers called "meteoric success" as a director, I'm not in the business of making a quick name for myself or a quick buck,' he explained. 'What I want to do is to direct plays and films which satisfy me and which I can feel proud of.' He looked at his watch. 'I must be off.'

'Go now,' she told him as he started to clear away the pots.

Keir grinned. 'Thanks.' He was halfway to the door when he stopped. 'We'll do the tying scene when I come back. All right?'

'Fine,' she agreed.

She stacked the plates in the dishwasher, wiped around, and went into the living-room. Picking up the paperback that she was reading, she plopped herself down in the corner of the sofa. As she found her page she smiled. Now that she knew Keir was not as mercenary as she had imagined and that his evenings had been spent editing and not with another woman, she felt so much better.

Keir stood facing her, alongside the bed. It was almost ten o'clock, and dark. The bedside lamp had been switched on, casting a single pool of golden light in the shadowy room.

'If I clasp your shoulders, twist you around and drop you on to the bed, then I can sit alongside. I grab your wrists and wrap the scarf around them,' he muttered, moving his hands as he mapped out the action. 'Then, I lift——'

'No,' Darcy said. Reaching out, she spread her fingers around his upper arms, gripped tight and heaved.

'What are you doing?' Keir protested, but, taken by surprise, he was already half stumbling back and half being pushed down on to the bed.

As he collapsed she swept the long chiffon scarf from the table, hopped over him and knelt. The scarf was wound around his wrists. A moment later his arms were yanked above his head and a knot secured.

'I'm tying you to the bed-rails,' she said, grinning triumphantly down at him. 'And it works.'

He frowned. 'Does it?'

'Yes! You never expected to find yourself flat on your back and neither would anyone else, so it has shock value. And don't you see,' she carried on, 'Anna tying Marcus not only shows that she wants to capture him emotionally, because she's already in thrall, but the image of a girl tying a six-foot-four man to a bed is one which the audience'll "take home, remember and *think about*"? Trust me,' Darcy said.

'I trust you about as far as I can throw you, which,' Keir said, with a droll, upward glance at where his wrists were bound to the brass rails, 'is not too far just now. However, you're right.'

'You agree we should play the scene this way?'

'I do.'

'Even though it's not what the writer may have intended?'

'It's better,' he said.

Darcy laughed out loud. The idea had come to her earlier in the evening as she had sat and read, and it had seemed so appropriate. So right.

'Thank you, thank you,' she burbled, and, carried away by her delight, she bent over and kissed him.

The magic was instant. Her lips parted on his, their tongues meshed and the kiss began in earnest. It was no ordinary kiss. It went on and on, and when it finished it led straight into another. Darcy was placing a hand on either side of his head to steady herself when he said something against her mouth.

'Sorry?' she asked, drawing back on to her haunches to gaze at him with dazed green eyes.

'Untie me. You can't keep me strung up forever,' he said. 'I need to undress you.'

'Un—undress me?' she faltered.

'And myself.' His voice became husky. 'Unless you want to do it?'

Darcy's heart fluttered. She had never undressed a man before and the idea of removing his clothes thrilled and scared her in equal proportions. It seemed enticingly brazen, but suppose she fumbled it?

'Um . . .' she said.

Keir's gaze narrowed. 'You're not thinking of making another quick exit? Of starting and stopping again?' he protested. With a powerful downward pull he wrenched on his tied wrists. The brass rails reverberated, there was the sound of material tearing and a moment later Darcy was manhandled down on to the bed. Lying alongside her, he plunged his fingers into the richness of dark hair at the back of her head and pulled her close. 'Darcy, you *can't*,' he said roughly, and kissed her.

The moist captivity of his mouth was stunning. The graze of his tongue made her head spin. She wound an arm around his neck and as he sipped at her lips Darcy felt her breasts grow heavy and her nipples tighten. When he started to undo the buttons on her dress she sighed. And helped him. Her dress and underwear swiftly disappeared.

Drawing back, Keir gazed down at her with heavy-lidded eyes as he feasted on the smooth curves and planes of her body which gleamed golden in the lamplight. 'I've waited so many years for this,' he murmured, and as he brushed his fingertips across the hardness of her nipples an avalanche of feeling swept over her.

He lowered his head and she felt his breath, warm against the taut globes of her breasts. Opening his mouth, he took in a tight peak and drew on it strongly. She writhed against him. Darcy heard someone cry out. Dear God, it was *her*. She struggled for control, for decorum, but when he drew on her nipple a second time, and a third, she cried out again.

She dragged at the buttons on his shirt. She needed to touch him, was desperate to feel his skin, wanted him naked against her.

'Careful,' Keir murmured, amused by her haste, and together they peeled off his shirt. 'Now my jeans,' he said.

The breath caught in her throat. 'Oh . . . yes.'

'You're shy?' he asked, smiling at her when she hesitated.

'No,' she vowed, but although her hands went to his belt it was Keir who unzipped the fly and shed his denims. And his underpants, which were white briefs.

He drew her against his chest and as she felt the touch and heat of his skin a primal need took hold. She moved against him, dragging the tips of her breasts over the mat of tawny curls and revelling in the scour.

'My highly sexed lady,' he murmured.

Was she highly sexed? Darcy wondered mistily. She had never thought so before, but now she was doing what came naturally and felt no inhibitions. With him she wanted to do everything, she thought impulsively.

He kissed her mouth, the smooth roundness of her shoulder, and eased himself lower to kiss her breasts.

'Don't stop,' she begged when, leaving her nipples swollen and deliciously sore, he eventually raised his head.

'But I want to kiss you here,' he said throatily, and his hand slid down over her hip-bone and between her thighs.

Teasingly and fleetingly his fingers played amid the moist tangles of dark hair and then his thumb found the tiny protruding beak of pink flesh. He caressed her and as Darcy submitted to the ecstasy her head rolled from side to side on the pillow.

'Now kiss me. There. Please,' she implored, and as he moved down her body and she felt the probe of his tongue in that most private of places she gasped.

'So beautifully responsive,' he murmured.

'Again,' Darcy whispered, amazed at her own daring but the victim of a wildly escalating need.

He tasted her again and she cried out. She was melting and dissolving, drowning in a whirlpool of pure pleasure.

In time Keir returned to lie on the pillow beside her. 'Touch me,' he said, and, taking hold of her hand, he carried it down his body.

As she felt the thrust of his maleness, the hard velvet muscle, the blood roared wildly in her head.

'God,' he muttered as she curled her fingers around him. 'Do you know what you're doing to me? Of course you do,' he said, and drew in a harsh breath. He slid his hand between her thighs again, a finger dipping inside her. 'So creamy, so ready,' he murmured.

'Please, now,' she implored, her eyes shut tight.

'You're taking precautions?'

Darcy opened her eyes. 'Precautions?' she repeated bemusedly.

'Are you on the Pill, using a cap?'

'Er . . . no.'

'So it's up to me,' Keir said, and reached for his jeans. He took out a packet. 'I don't like these damn things, but it's just as well I called into the drugstore.'

Her body aching and restless and in need, Darcy waited. 'Make love to me,' she insisted as soon as he was ready. She put her arms around him. 'Now.'

They kissed again and as the open-mouthed kisses continued and their breathing quickened Keir straddled her. 'Darcy . . .' he groaned, and she felt the fierce urgency of his body. He had started to move, when he abruptly halted. He pushed himself up on his arms. 'You're a virgin,' he protested, gazing down at her with stunned eyes.

'Yes,' she said simply.

'But it never occurred to me—— I felt sure—— That's why you weren't prepared,' he said in garbled confusion.

'You can't stop now. You *can't*,' Darcy implored, and lifted her hips.

Keir gave a low, anguished groan. He had been close to his climax and the slide of her body inexorably drew him towards it again. He could not resist.

'Honey,' he muttered as the needs of the flesh took control of him, and of her.

After years of waiting and wondering, and fantasising, the pain Darcy had imagined was slight—and swiftly absorbed by the urgency of her desire. Deftly, Keir led her on into greater pleasure, greater passion, greater abandonment. His rhythm increased.

'Now,' he said in a low, driven tone. 'Now.'

He possessed her and, a moment later, her climax erupted in a vast explosion of feeling which ran down her arms and legs, clenched at her heart and made her cry. She might have been unable to touch the moon at the museum, she thought in the dim recesses of her mind, but she had touched it now.

Keir held her close. 'Did I hurt you?' he asked anxiously. 'I tried not to.'

Darcy smiled at him through her tears. 'No. I'm crying because—because it was so wonderful. It was all I ever hoped for and more.'

'And for me,' he murmured. 'And for me.'

CHAPTER SEVEN

'So YOU didn't have an affair with Gideon McCall,' Keir said as they lay together, basking in the sweet lethargy which came after lovemaking. The blankets had been drawn up, to keep them warm as their bodies cooled and their heartbeats steadied.

'No, nor with anyone else,' Darcy said wryly, and sighed. 'I suppose I should explain.'

'Please.'

Pulling away a little so that she could look at him, she assembled her thoughts. 'When Gideon first asked me out I was sure I liked him,' she began, 'but——' she hesitated, wondering whether to reveal the whole truth, then deciding that such confidences could be left for later '—I soon realised that I didn't.

'However, he was convinced I adored him—Gideon's ego is such that he's convinced every female he meets must adore him,' she inserted drily, 'and when he tried to hustle me into bed and I said no way he was so peeved. He went off in a huff, rang a reporter, and proceeded to give him a lengthy interview in which he claimed that we were lovers.'

'I read it.'

'In that case you may remember how Gideon went into graphic detail about where our lovemaking was supposed to have occurred.'

'In a meadow, on the seashore, backstage at the theatre,' Keir said, exhibiting a surprising recall.

Darcy pulled a face. 'Yes. It was such a juicy story that all the other tabloids gobbled it up and had a field-day.'

'Being seen as the lover of Sir Rupert Weston's daughter wouldn't have done his image as a dreamboat or his career any harm,' he observed.

'None. Gideon wallowed in the fuss he'd created and squeezed it for every last drop of publicity, but I was mortified. I felt so exploited, so cheapened.' She winced at the memory. 'Reporters trailed me around for ages, asking for my version, but I refused to say a word.'

'You weren't inclined to tell them that it was a frame-up and complete fiction?'

'No. Perhaps I should've done, but I was desperate for the story to die and the best way to kill it off was to keep quiet. Besides, I was almost the only virgin I knew even *then*,' Darcy said with dry emphasis, 'and if the general belief was that I'd slept with Gideon McCall that stopped it from becoming an issue.'

'Was Gideon aware of your virginity?' Keir enquired.

'No, but I was afraid that if I announced that he was lying the papers might speculate about it——' she winced again '—and I had visions of them tagging me with a "virgin" label and making a big event out of who might relieve me of it.'

His brows tilted down a notch. 'And because Gideon was reckoned to have bedded you it was assumed that subsequent boyfriends did too.'

'Yes, and that's how any myth of my being——' Darcy shot him a look '—fast and loose began.'

'I didn't think you were fast and loose,' Keir protested, bending to press a kiss to her shoulder. He grinned. 'I just thought you were headstrong and incredibly experienced.' His expression sobered. 'You've never fallen for anyone?' he enquired.

'Sometimes a little, but not enough to sleep with them. I realise this may seem old-fashioned and out-of-step for someone who's an actress, but I find the idea of hopping into bed with different people and going from one affair to the next pretty shallow.' Her eyes clouded. 'Also, it virtually always means that somewhere along the way someone's bound to get hurt.'

'You believe in love and marriage, and being faithful ever after?'

'I do,' she said firmly.

'Rupert's behaviour has had a hell of an effect,' Keir remarked, 'one way and another.'

Darcy stiffened. 'I beg your pardon?'

'If you've resisted lovemaking for this long and are so scared of affairs—which in my experience are not all shallow—then it's obvious that his slack morals have severely hurt *you*.'

She drew back from the circle of his arms. She found the term 'slack morals' offensive, even though it was an accurate description of her father's conduct and although she had vowed that she would never behave in such a manner herself. But... But...

Her mind jerked. Realisation stabbed like the steel blade of a stiletto. They had made no commitment and had a relationship which was, to say the least, rocky, so, in sleeping with him, wasn't she guilty of slack morals herself?

Her head began to pound. When concocting her seduction scheme she had never intended to go so far as to give herself to Keir, Darcy thought despairingly, but that was what she had done. Her blood ran cold. She had given herself to the man who had lethally harmed her father.

How could she have been so disloyal and unthinking, she wondered, so wrapped up in her own pleasure and so carried away? Of all the men on earth, what had possessed her to make love, and for that very first, treasured time, with *him*?

Diving down, Darcy grabbed her bra from the floor, shoved her arms through the straps and fastened the hooks behind her back. A moment ago she had imagined them making love again and sleeping wrapped around each other all through the night, but no longer. Not now that it was infamously clear that this was a second bedroom incident which had been a tragic mistake.

Darcy flung back the covers. 'And *you* hurt Rupert,' she countered fiercely.

As he had watched her scramble into action with surprise, Keir had pushed himself up against the pillow. 'Excuse me?' he said.

'You hated him,' she declared, leaping out to pull on her bikini briefs.

'I didn't. OK, like you I was no admirer of his promiscuous lifestyle, but the guy was a charmer and a talented, industrious actor and——'

'Forget the soft soap,' Darcy snapped. Her dress was being dragged on and the buttons feverishly fastened. 'You tyrannised him.'

Keir moved long fingers over his chest, circling the mat of dark blond curls. The movement appeared idle and pensive, yet his blue eyes were alert. The lethargy they had been sharing had gone.

'I did what?' he enquired, quietly but with bite.

'Rupert never admitted it, but when he withdrew from the play he was agitated and depressed. It was obvious that he'd taken an exceedingly hard knock and he'd taken it from you.'

'You're saying his...agitation was my fault?' he demanded.

'I am.' Darcy wished that he would stop circling his chest. The brush of his fingers was reminding her of how it had felt when she had brushed the tips of her breasts across the wiry hair. It had felt like bliss.

'Until he worked with you my father had always been a happy and confident character, even if he did have "slack morals",' she squeezed out thinly, 'but afterwards he was a different man. He moped around, showing no interest in anything—not even in his career, which had been of such vital importance to him. He became more anguished and remote until——' a painful lump formed in her throat and her voice broke '—he walked in front of the bus.'

'Rupert walked under a bus?' Keir said sharply. 'I didn't know that. I was on location in Brazil with a film I was directing at the time, and it was only on my return a couple of months later that someone told me he'd been killed in a road accident, but I assumed he'd been in a car.'

'Driving it?' Darcy enquired.

'Yes. Rupert did tend to be erratic at the wheel, especially after sampling the wine, and——'

'You assumed it was his fault. It wasn't. Not at all.' She took a breath as the grievance which had festered inside her for seven long years finally broke loose and burst out. 'It was *yours*!'

A pulse throbbed beneath the tanned skin of his temple. 'Mine?'

'The official verdict was accidental death because my father hadn't looked where he was going, but I think that by that time he damn near wanted to die and——' Darcy was spitting out the words '—you killed him!'

'That's not true,' he said heavily.

'You're the one who caused his unhappiness and so, while you may not have actually raised two hands, you pushed him out into the road.'

Keir's lips tightened into a harsh line. 'You're wrong.'

'Am I?' Darcy demanded, glaring at him. Earlier, as she had remembered the tragedy of her father's death, she had almost cried, but now she was using the white flame of her anger to keep the tears at bay. 'I think not.'

'Think again,' he commanded, climbing from between the sheets to pull on his clothes. 'Have I tyrannised you or any of the other actors in the play? Have you heard talk of me tyrannising anyone in the past?'

'No, but——'

'And in our business dark gossip often leaks. Correct?'

'Yes, but——'

'The reason you've heard no gossip, no talk, is because I don't tyrannise,' he said, the flare of his nostrils indicating his acute distaste for the word. 'I never have, ever, and never will.'

'I may not have had sightings of you in the actual throes, or be able to produce any witnesses who are prepared to take the stand——' she began icily.

'None,' he barked.

'—but my father suffered. He was in good health physically, but mentally he became a ruin. Thanks to you!'

Keir tucked his shirt into his jeans and drew up the zip. 'It's all circumstantial,' he said as he fastened the buckle on his black leather belt, 'but if that's what you want to believe so be it.'

'You've stopped defending yourself?' she taunted.

'I have.'

Darcy's mouth twisted with derision. 'That didn't take long.'

'I've stopped because you're so bloody blinkered,' he rasped, 'and because I happen to believe that people are innocent until proven guilty.'

'Although I lack concrete proof it was a point of honour with Rupert never to let anyone down and I know, I can *guarantee*, that he would never have withdrawn from the production at the last moment unless he'd been desperate.' She flung out a furious and condemning arm. 'You caused his desperation.'

'Wrong,' he said, 'but you should use this anger in the play.'

Darcy blinked. 'What?'

'You want Anna to be tough? Go ahead, make her tough. Make her angry. Getting all this bottled-up emotion out of your system on stage will act as a safety-valve and be therapeutic.'

She gave him a long, cold stare. 'Is the play the only thing you ever think about?' she asked frigidly.

'No.' Pushing his hands into the pockets of his jeans, Keir stood with his long legs set apart. 'Something else that I'm thinking about—what I'm wondering about right now,' he said in a low, clipped voice, 'is why the hell did you make love with me if you believe I'm such a bastard?'

Darcy felt a tide of colour wash up her face. She supposed that the question had been inevitable, though that did not make it any easier to answer.

'Isn't it obvious?' she said, holding her head up high and refusing to shrink from his gaze. 'I wanted to get rid of my virginity. If it was embarrassing at eighteen, to be saddled with it at twenty-five was damn near ridiculous——' she pealed out a merry laugh '—so I decided I must lose it.'

'And you've been kissing me so enthusiastically in order to put me in the mood?'

Her shoulders rose and fell. 'What else?'

'But why choose me?' he demanded, his blue eyes intense beneath their heavy brows.

'Because you were someone I knew and because I guessed you'd be an experienced and controlled lover,' Darcy replied, with a gloriously offhand smile. 'And you were. As you know, you made my first time a wonderful occasion. So thanks.'

'Get out,' Keir said.

'Sorry?'

'Get out of here. Get out of my sight. Go to bed,' he grated, his face as black as thunder. 'You think you can use me and I won't care? I do. I care about being *teased*——' the word was a condemnation of her malpractice, a grievous slur '—and I object to being turned into a damn gigolo!

'What comes next? You tuck a wad of dollar bills gratefully into my hip pocket, or how about enrolling me to teach you the finer points of lovemaking in six easy lessons? Not that you need much teaching,' he said, with a curl of his lips. 'You seem to manage fine all by yourself.'

Darcy eyed him warily. While she refused to be intimidated, it was clear that in attempting to make light of their lovemaking she had been *too* flippant.

'Look, I'm——' she began, but got no further.

'Go!' Keir thundered. 'I may be a controlled lover——' the look he thrust her dripped contempt like battery acid '—but the hold I have on my emotions right now is extremely precarious.'

Darcy turned and walked silently out of the room. All those years ago at the Brierly Hotel she had left of her own free will, she recalled as she made her way along the landing, but this time, with a soul-battering vice versa symmetry, it was Keir who had ejected her.

'More coffee?' The voice floated on the outer edges of her consciousness. 'I said, would you care for some more coffee, miss?' the voice asked again, impatiently this time.

Darcy looked up in surprise. A waitress in an orange and white polyester overall, and holding a glass jug of steaming black coffee, was standing over her.

'Oh. Yes. Please,' she said hastily, realising from a quick glance round the table that everyone else had already had their cups refilled.

It was the following day and Darcy had gone with the rest of the cast for lunch at the local diner. She had not felt particularly hungry—indeed, her appetite seemed to have almost disappeared—but she had been afraid that if she stayed alone to work out at the theatre Saul might pick up the wrong signal, decide that she had changed her mind and attempt to corral her again.

However, by choosing a seat well away and excluding her from his conversation, the young man had made *his* signal abundantly clear—his pursuit was not to be renewed.

As Darcy added cream to her coffee, and as her colleagues ate and chatted around her, she returned to her thoughts. She had been recalling how, when she had gone

down to breakfast that morning, she had been ready for
Keir to order her to get out of his house.

'You want me to take myself off to a Holiday Inn?'
she had enquired when she'd joined him at the table
where he had been eating a muffin.

'No need,' he'd replied.

'But I'm not exactly your favourite guest,' she'd said,
noting that, while his manner was formal and abrupt,
his fury of the previous evening had thankfully receded,
or was under tighter control.

'Even so, you can stay.'

'You're afraid that if you send me packing I might
ignore the Holiday Inn, and your wrath, and book into
the De Robillard again?' Darcy had suggested.

He had slung her a dark look. 'That hadn't occurred
to me, though it seems just the kind of bloody-minded
thing you would do. You don't feel inclined to move out
yourself?' Keir had continued.

'No. My bedroom's comfortable,' she'd said, a touch
airily. 'Having a chauffeur to take me to and from rehearsals saves any bother of taxis——'

'Nice to know I'm useful,' he'd muttered.

'—and our day-to-day living works smoothly, or it has
until now.'

Keir had accepted her statement with a terse nod.

Darcy cast a look down to the other end of the table,
where her host was explaining to Thea how instead of
expending all her energy in an early big scene it would
be wiser to pace herself.

If Keir was willing for her to remain, albeit reluc-
tantly, then it seemed that he would not subject her to
too much of the deep-freeze treatment or be overly ag-
gressive. As far as the practicalities were concerned they
would carry on as before. She bit into a slice of cu-

cumber from the green salad which she had picked at and left. She could live with that.

Last night's events had meant the end of her seduction of Keir, she reflected as she chewed, though now it was startlingly clear that what had seemed so credible and clever when she had dreamed it up had not been one of her better ideas. On the contrary, it ranked as pure loony tunes. She should have realised that he was not the kind of man who would be manipulated and she ought to have guessed that her hormones were destined to send the situation cartwheeling into chaos.

Exactly how far had she intended to go? Darcy wondered. When she had planned to come on strong in New York, what had she had in mind? She did not know, because she had never properly thought through the mad-fool scheme.

Her revenge had collapsed—and with it any hope of finding out what had happened between Keir and her father. Darcy sighed. Keir had accused her of being blinkered, yet about what?

Admittedly, her adoration of her father had been all-inclusive when he was alive, but since her mother's death she had been acknowledging, though only to herself, that he had had faults and much to answer for. Rupert had been nowhere near the ideal father—or husband, or lover either—yet where his profession had been concerned he had always been co-operative and reliable.

She looked down the length of the table again. If Keir had nothing to hide and nothing to be ashamed of, why wouldn't he tell her the truth? It was his refusal to explain which damned him as guilty.

Her gaze narrowed. Thea had an arm hooped around his neck and was smoothing down the thick dark blond hair at the back of his head. She cringed. The woman was overdoing it. She looked around their group, expecting to see other cringes, but no one else seemed to have noticed.

'Everyone finished?' Keir enquired, suddenly pushing back his chair. There was a collective affirmative. 'Then let's get back to work.'

On the short walk back to the theatre Darcy chatted at first with the two middle-aged actors, but as one went off to have a word with Thea, and the other roped himself into a conversation between Saul and the elderly actress, the structure of the little procession changed and she found herself walking alongside Keir.

'You enjoy being stroked?' she enquired, shooting him a sideways look.

'Stroked?' he asked.

'By Thea. She was all over you at lunch, though that's nothing new. I've noticed how she never misses a chance to sidle close and fondle, but then I suppose you must appeal to her maternal instincts.'

'Miaow,' he said, and lifted a brow. 'Are you jealous?'

'Me, jealous?' Darcy gave a hoot of derision. 'Fat chance. What an idea. P-lease.'

'The classic retort,' he said, 'but who are you trying to convince—me or yourself?'

Darcy glowered. What she needed to do was come back with some stinging reply which would chop him metaphorically off at the knees, but to her irritation she could not think of anything.

'No, I don't enjoy being stroked,' Keir continued, looking ahead at where the older actress was safely out of earshot. 'In fact it sets my teeth on edge, but I accept it because I don't know how to get Thea to stop, short of telling her to leave me alone, which could upset her.

And if she's to do her best in the play I don't want her to be upset.'

'Which means that, yet again, you consider most things are acceptable so long as they help the production,' Darcy said astringently.

There was a pause as if he might have been making himself count to ten before he answered her jibe. 'I guess you could say that,' he agreed with careful equanimity.

They had broken off rehearsals in the middle of a scene which included their characters plus the two older men, and on returning to the theatre the action was picked up where it had been left off. The scene progressed, slowly and surely, and, in time, the actors made their exits and the two of them were alone. As the rest of the cast watched from the wings Keir said his lines and Darcy responded.

'Then there's a kiss,' she rattled off dismissively, 'and next I say——'

'We'll do it,' he instructed.

Darcy looked at him with startled green eyes. 'Do it?' she echoed, thrown by his volte-face and abrupt change of routine.

She had felt certain that his anger over being used would have had him not only continuing to ignore their clinches in rehearsal but now delaying them until the last possible moment. She had believed that touching her in any way, shape or form would no longer appeal.

'I want to see how the various pieces of lovemaking fit into the rhythm of the play,' Keir said, and pulled her into his arms.

Darcy had expected him to simulate the kiss, but as his mouth pressed against hers his lips parted and she felt the thrust of his tongue. A predatory thrust. A giddying thrust. Surprised, she started to draw back—but his arm tightened around her, keeping her close.

She frowned up at him. 'What——?' she began in confusion.

'Try and stop me,' he said quietly, challenge glittering in his blue eyes, and his head bent again and his mouth covered hers.

Although she hesitated for a moment, Darcy did not to try to stop him. What was the point? Not only was he far stronger and, if she resisted, could easily force her, but, with the other actors looking on, she was unwilling to start an argument.

If they argued there seemed a chance that Keir, with his anger and his direct approach to sexual matters, might throw out a comment about their making love the previous night, and she did not want it made public. No, thanks. But also—a crucial also—his lips and his tongue were druggingly persuasive.

Cursing herself for being so damn susceptible, Darcy slid her arms up around his neck. The kiss was long and deep and devout, and when he finally released her her heart was thumping and her legs were shaky. She felt as if she had been freefalling through space.

She was gamely if breathlessly starting off into her next lines when the sound of clapping erupted from the side of the stage. Surprised, she glanced round and saw Thea frowning and Saul with a cynical, 'I knew it' look on his face, while the other three cast members were jovially applauding.

'Bravo,' cheered the elderly actress.

'Now that's what I term authentic,' called one of the middle-aged actors.

'You guys are sure spicing things up,' hollered the other, and laughed.

Darcy replied with a taut smile. As far as she was concerned the kiss had been no laughing matter. It wasn't funny at all.

Nor were the ones in the days which followed, for Keir had decreed that they would act out every clinch and kiss, and whenever they did he made it for real.

It wasn't clear whether it was because they were in front of others or because she had forfeited her previous attraction, but each time Keir remained unmoved, whereas Darcy became more aroused. So often he took her close to the limit, to a point where she felt she must cry out, where she had to abandon her grasp on the play, but he seemed to know exactly where her limit was and always drew her back.

As the weeks of rehearsals rolled into the technical rehearsal at the commercial theatre, then into dress rehearsals, over and over again Darcy vowed that she would rebel and make the *next* kiss a sham. Why should she be coerced? From now on she was not going to cooperate. But each time her resolve faded beneath the tantalising pressure of his lips.

It was true that at the dress rehearsals, when seats had been filled, her reaction had been tempered. The audiences had acted like a bodyguard and a welcome restraint, and were destined to do so in future, yet dreading Keir's kisses—and longing for them—was like bouncing on a knife-edge.

'I must thank you,' Keir said as they walked across the parking ground at the rear of the theatre and towards the stage door.

The play opened tonight. This evening, and for all the other performances of the Washington run, seats were almost completely sold out. Whether this had anything to do with the comments which Herbie Krantz had dropped into his column about 'coy' Darcy Weston sharing the comforts of 'virile' Keir Robards' home it was impossible to tell. However, they might have boosted interest and been a useful plug, for in New York the ticket sales were far less healthy.

'Thank me for what?' Darcy enquired.

'For stopping Thea from stroking me. You hadn't noticed that she doesn't do it any more?' he said when she frowned.

'No,' she replied, thinking that these days her awareness of him, combined with her concentration on the play, seemed to have transcended almost everything else. 'But how have I stopped her?'

'Thea said she hadn't realised until we started on the clinches that there was something going on between us, and although at one time she'd hoped she and I might've become an item she's abandoned the idea. Which is why she and Saul are . . . fraternising.'

Darcy's brows lifted in surprise. 'They are?'

'With gusto. So he must enjoy being stroked, despite Thea's vast age,' Keir added drily.

They had arrived at the theatre early, and as Keir went off to have a final word with the stage manager Darcy walked along to her dressing-room. Now that they had moved into the proper theatre, and because she played the lead, she had been allocated a room of her own.

As she sat trying to calm her first-night nerves, and reading through the fax messages and good-luck cards which Maurice and relations and friends had sent, her thoughts wandered back to Keir. He had once said something about it being a jungle out there, but to her it seemed as if the jungle was all around and she was living with a tiger—a handsome tawny tiger who had prowled back into her life mercilessly to maul at her emotions.

She started to do her make-up. So many nights she had lain awake wondering whether Keir might prowl from his bed and into hers. She had wondered—and hoped.

Picking up a lip pencil, she outlined the shape of her mouth. It might have been madness, but she wanted him to make love to her again. Just as her character, Anna, was supposed to be desperate with longing, so was she. She seemed to have a chasm of yearning inside her which ached to be filled.

But, in the same way she had earlier restricted their kisses to the kissing demanded by the play, so now had Keir. He was punishing her and making her pay. She stared at her reflection in the mirror. It was the biter bit.

'Listen to this one, guys,' Thea yelled excitedly, but the rest of the cast, plus assorted partners, were too busy poring over other reviews in first morning editions of other newspapers to pay any attention.

The atmosphere in the private room at a prominent Washington restaurant, which Cal Warburg had reserved for a post-show supper, was boisterous with celebration. Just as a few hours earlier the deafening applause when the curtain had come down had demonstrated the audience's appreciation, now the glowing praise of the critics confirmed that the play *had* been theatrical dynamite.

Or, to be exact, Darcy thought cautiously as her eyes absorbed yet more sentences of adulation, it was deemed so in Washington. But success could be a dodgy business and the response in New York—where it really mattered—could be different.

Putting down the paper, she grinned. New York lay in the future and for now she felt deliriously happy and weak with relief. All the weeks of hard work had paid off. The expending of so much nervous energy had been worthwhile and a goodly proportion of her energy had gone into making Anna tough. Drawing on past grievances, she had added a weight, a crackle, to her character.

She was thinking that maybe this had been therapeutic, as Keir had vowed, when Thea, who was sitting beside her, shrilled out again.

'"Riveting performances all around,"' she shrieked, determined to be heard, '"including the always bewitching Thea Crosby——"' the actress paused to beam '"—and especially from Keir Robards and Darcy Weston. The strength Miss Weston gives to her character contains an undertow of insecurity which tugs at the heart,"' she read. '"Her fragile yet feisty beauty makes the perfect foil for Keir Robards' solid power, and their unsparing portrayals will linger in the mind for a long time to come."'

'Purple prose,' Darcy said, with a smile. 'Yet music to the ears.'

'Wait for it,' Thea said, her eyes dancing. '"And oh, the sexual chemistry between them!"'

Darcy chose to ignore the remark. 'The part about insecurity——' she began.

'Is true. Don't ask me to explain it, but the stronger you made Anna, the more vulnerable you made her too. *So-o* effective.' Thea cast a glance to the other side of the table, where a man who Darcy had been informed was a leading senator was energetically shaking Keir's hand. 'And our director knew that.'

'You did a great job, Darcy,' proclaimed Cal Warburg, who was sitting on the other side of her. He raised his glass of champagne. 'I'm indebted.'

She grinned. The producer was a friendly, balding, bespectacled man in his mid-fifties. Before the performance he and his wife had sent baskets of flowers, accompanied by their best wishes, to every member of the cast. They had been overwhelmed by the play—'And I don't usually care for straight things, just musicals,' the pear-shaped Mrs Warburg had cheerfully confessed—and were now wholeheartedly joining in the junketing.

'Thank you,' Darcy said, 'but it was a team effort.'

'A truly gifted team,' Cal Warburg declared, and, rising to his feet and demanding quiet, he proceeded to toast everyone exuberantly. 'The milk of paradise must be flowing through your veins,' he said to Keir, who had received his special praise.

Keir gave a throaty chuckle. 'Bollinger, I think.'

More effusive reviews were read out, more champagne was drunk, what seemed like a continuous queue of people came and went, offering their congratulations. The senator, who zeroed in on Darcy, spent a long time showering her with compliments.

The night wore on, the rush of adrenalin gradually slowed and goodnights started to be said. Darcy was looking at Keir, who had been trapped by yet another well-wisher, and hoping that they could leave soon, when she was aware of someone sliding into the chair which Thea had vacated.

'You lied,' the person said, and when she turned she saw Herbie Krantz.

'Sorry?'

'You told me that you and Keir weren't having a fling.'

I wish we were, Darcy thought. Oh, heavens, how I wish we were. 'We're not,' she said flatly.

The reporter cocked his head. No matter what he wrote in his columns he prided himself on being able to recognise the truth when he heard it—and he heard it now.

'But you love the guy,' he protested, for he was also a closet romantic.

Darcy rested her elbow on the table, her chin on her hand. 'I was acting,' she said tiredly. 'My character is supposed to love his character and——'

'Doll, every time you look at him, whether it's at rehearsals or on stage or here this evening, you give the game away. You love Keir Robards.'

'But——' she started to argue.

'Believe it.'

Hours later as she lay in bed, exhausted and spent yet unable to sleep, Darcy thought about what Herbie Krantz had said. Her heart cramped. He was right. She believed him. She did love Keir; she had loved him seven years ago and now it seemed that she'd never stopped.

Darcy stared bleakly out into the shadowy, moonlit room. Had she gone from boyfriend to boyfriend because she had been looking for, yet had never found, someone like him? Might she have guarded her virginity for so long because subconsciously she had been saving herself for Keir? Had she decided on her seduction strategy as an excuse to get near? It seemed so. She *knew* so.

With a shuddering sob she pushed her face into the pillow. Keir claimed not to have tyrannised her father, but now, with his so sensual, so sham, so public kisses— and because she loved him—he was tyrannising *her*.

CHAPTER EIGHT

'THAT was Cal Warburg on the phone,' Keir reported, coming back into the kitchen where, at a table strewn with the remnants of a meal and several Sunday papers, they were finishing a lazy late breakfast. 'Apparently the surge in advance bookings which the rave reviews here produced has ground to a halt and so the situation in New York is still——' he tilted a large hand '—iffy.'

Darcy helped herself to a last slice of wholemeal toast. 'But there's another week to go before we transfer,' she protested, 'and once we're up and running word of mouth is bound to sell more seats.'

'Some. However, if we're to do much better than break even it looks as though we're going to need a resounding thumbs-up from the Axe Man.' He frowned. 'And the play certainly couldn't survive his thumbs-down.'

'Not a chance,' she acknowledged with a grimace.

The Axe Man was the nickname of the journalist who was the most read, the most listened-to and the most powerful critic on Broadway. He inspired fear and trepidation in the hearts of the hardiest of stage professionals, for his word ranked as law with the majority of New York's theatregoers and thus his word could make or break a show. And, Darcy reflected ruefully, the sometimes bombastic gentleman had broken good ones.

'It seems wrong to me that a production should be so much at the mercy of one person's opinion,' she remarked as she spread the toast with black cherry jam. 'In London and, so far as I know, in other major cities

157

the reviewing scene's more diverse and no single critic has such a vital casting vote.'

'It's unfair,' Keir agreed, pulling his chair out from the table and sitting down again. 'But on Broadway the Axe Man reigns supreme, so all we can do is hope we catch him on a good night and that he's as bowled over by the show as everyone else.'

At his words Darcy heard the tiny ring of an alarm bell. And what I hope, she added silently, is that I don't mess things up.

After a week when she had felt that each time she played her part she had played it a satisfying little bit better, the previous evening she had hit a bad moment. In the middle of the second act all of a sudden she had forgotten her lines. Completely. A wall of terror had seemed to come down inside her head, she had stood mute and frantic, but a second later the lines had returned. No one had noticed—not Keir, nor the other actors, or the audience.

Such a lapse had never happened to her before—and please, God, Darcy thought fervently, it never would again. Though why should it? She knew her lines inside out and back to front. She could if necessary recite them standing on her head. No, the momentary amnesia had been a one-time blip. There was no reason to panic.

'Do you want to stay around here for the rest of the day or would you like to take in some more sights?' Keir enquired when final cups of coffee had been drunk and breakfast was over. 'I'm happy to drive you.'

'What do you want to do?' she asked.

He slowly stretched, his torso taut and, she found herself visualising, bronzed beneath the pale grey T-shirt; his elbows bent, then his long arms languorously straightened. He was like an idle tiger stirring from its rest, she thought.

'I'm easy,' he said.

Darcy's heart pinched. When Keir wasn't tyrannising her with his kisses he *was* easy—to be with, to live with, to love.

'I'd like to visit the Lincoln Memorial and go on to the White House,' she declared, deciding that a trip out would help divert her thoughts from him—and from that curious loss of words.

Although Darcy had assured herself that the lapse would not be repeated, and on the Monday evening she was fine, on Tuesday it happened again. Perhaps it was because at the back of her mind she was thinking how awful it would be if she dried in front of an audience that had come primed to expect something extra special, but suddenly she was aware of hundreds of people looking at *her*, of her being the focal point of a multitude of eyes.

The lines went. Her spine trembled, her stomach began to shake, and almost immediately the lines reappeared. Whew! Yet for the rest of the performance she felt as if they might vanish again and that she was never more than a few words away from a gaping abyss.

Now painfully aware that she could forget, Darcy spent Wednesday giving herself private pep talks and psyching herself up. But as the play progressed that evening a pressure-cooker feeling built inside her, and in the next to last scene her mind emptied. Trapped in a waking nightmare, she stood paralysed and yet the muscles in her throat kept on working and she heard herself saying words—the correct words—with feeling. It was amazing...and bizarre.

When the curtain fell all she wanted to do was rush off to her dressing-room alone, curl up into a ball and plaintively *rock*. Instead she smiled as she took bow after bow, later signed autographs for people at the stage door, and, clinging desperately on to what had shredded down to the last tatters of calm, drove back to Georgetown with Keir.

'I'm going to bed,' Darcy declared the minute they walked in the door.

They usually sat for a while, he with a brandy and she nursing a mug of hot chocolate, chatting idly about the show as they came down from their highs, unwound and so would be able to sleep. But tonight, sunk in her slough of despond, she was in no mood for chattering, or relaxing, and, she felt certain, was doomed to toss and turn wretchedly until dawn.

'What's the matter?' Keir asked.

'I'm tired.' Darcy yawned as if to provide proof, and took a step towards the stairs. 'It's late so——'

'No, I mean what was the matter this evening? And yesterday evening.' Taking off his black blazer, he slung it over one shoulder—an action which even in her misery registered as being fetchingly elegant. 'You've stopped giving yourself up to the play. You're holding back.'

Darcy stood very still. While Keir had not recognised the real problem, he knew that something had gone amiss. But she was reluctant to admit to incompetence and be seen as inept. Besides, she would cure her forgetfulness. Tomorrow. She would. She would.

A laugh was prised out. 'Boloney,' she said.

'You're holding back,' Keir reiterated, 'and if you do you'll weaken the meaning of the play, the impact.'

She bridled. The audience's prolonged applause had shown that they had been impressed by her performance, she thought defiantly, and after the strains of the evening the last thing she needed was for him to start to criticise and carp.

'I'm turning it into a piece of hokum?' she demanded, with chin lifted.

'Of course not,' he said impatiently, 'but——'

'And, if I should, what do you intend to do—lynch me?' Darcy enquired. The question had been haughty and chill, but without warning her defiance snapped. Her lower lip quivered. Tears filled her eyes. She felt crushed and beaten. 'I can't help it!' she wailed.

'Hey,' Keir protested. Tossing his jacket over a hook, he strode forward as if intending to enfold her in his arms—but a yard away he stopped dead. Frowning, he pushed his hands into his trouser pockets. 'What's wrong?' he asked.

So it was no more Mr Nice Guy, Darcy thought wistfully. She supposed that she could not blame him for spurning any contact between them, though she longed to cling, to sob against his shoulder, to have him murmur soothing words.

She sniffed. 'I keep forgetting my lines,' she said, and chokily explained how her mind had gone blank. 'It's happened three times now and I don't understand why.'

'It's stage fright,' Keir told her.

Darcy looked at him in surprise. The idea was novel ... and yet so obvious. 'I suppose it must be,' she agreed.

'But it'll pass.'

'It might not. It won't. I know what's going to happen,' she whimpered, looking at him with huge, fraught eyes. 'I'll dry when we get to New York—on the first night when the Axe Man's there ... and he'll chop the play into little pieces ... and we'll have to close ... and everyone'll be thrown out of work...and it'll be all my fault.'

'This *is* boloney. I'm going to make us our drinks,' Keir continued, speaking calmly, 'and we'll talk.'

'There's no point in talking. All right, I've managed to say the lines so far, or at least my vocal cords have recited them even if my brain didn't know them, but——'

'Darcy, pack it in!' he commanded.

She released the air from her lungs in a ragged rush. 'I'm sorry,' she said. 'I don't usually go so crinkle-cut.'

Keir grinned at her. 'We all have our moments. Hot chocolate as usual?'

'Yes, please,' she said, and went with him, first to the kitchen where he prepared their drinks, and then through into the living-room.

'I think I might give up acting,' she mused as she sat at one end of the sofa with her legs tucked beneath her. She took a sip of chocolate. 'Not immediately——'

'Thank heavens,' Keir cut in, pulling a reluctant smile from her.

'—but perhaps when this play has ended.'

'Darcy, you're trained to act, you're real good at it, and it's all you've ever done.' He drank from his brandy goblet. 'And you're only saying this because you're in a slump and feeling scared.'

'Maybe, though I think it's more than that. I honestly don't believe I'd miss acting too much and giving up would solve all kinds of problems.' She put her thoughts of leaving the profession to one side. 'You said the stage fright will pass.'

'It will, but until it does you have to learn to deal with it.'

'How?' she asked.

Keir looked at her along the length of the sofa. 'First, you have to remember that if you should dry it doesn't mean the end of the civilised world as we know it. Neither are you performing brain surgery. Indeed, while this may bruise your ego, and while it tends to be a little-known fact among many of the denizens of the theatre,' he added drolly, 'in the scale of importance on planet earth acting doesn't come all that high.'

'My ego isn't bruised,' she said. 'I'd throw the actor out of the lifeboat before the doctor any day, and out before many other people.'

His mouth curved. 'That sounds healthy. And if you do dry,' he continued, 'you don't freak out.'

'No?'

'No, you waffle for a while—hell, no one's word-perfect all of the time—or, if the dialogue still remains elusive, why not burst into song or dance? You're trained in all kinds of stagecraft and Anna's headstrong, right?' he said when she looked at him in astonishment. 'So you and she are able to do anything.'

'I can tap-dance up a storm,' Darcy said, laughing, 'but if I did it'd throw the rest of you.'

'Into a flat spin,' he agreed. 'I'm not advocating that you should. The point I'm trying to make is that the creative imagination is a wonderful thing and you possess plenty of it, so, if the words should go, there are ways of giving yourself time to remember—if someone else doesn't come to your aid, which chances are they will do. Though you could sing a song in your head,' he carried on. 'Something familiar that'll relieve the tension and revive the memory.'

'Do you?' Darcy enquired, intrigued.

'I've never suffered from stage fright. Yet. But it happens to the best and most seasoned of performers.

And when it does it can cause one hell of a personal crisis.' Keir paused for a moment, pleating his lower lip with his fingers and frowning at her. 'However, I reckon that given time and a sensible approach it's curable.'

'By singing in your head?' she teased.

'And by knowing that everyone is rooting for you.' Seeing that she had finished her drink, he drained his brandy. 'Time for bed. Have a good night's sleep,' he said as they got up from the sofa, 'and everything'll seem better in the morning.'

She slid him a suddenly uncertain look. 'Promise?'

Keir smiled. 'I promise,' he said.

Walking ahead of him, Darcy went through the hall and up the stairs. When they reached the landing her step slowed. She was intending to bid him goodnight, but before she had a chance to turn she felt Keir's hand slide beneath the heavy fall of hair at the back of her neck and draw it to one side. A moment later his lips pressed against the warm softness of the scented skin which he had revealed.

Darcy stood rigid. His kiss was searing her flesh, causing every nerve-end to tingle, making her pulses race. Why couldn't he spin her around and kiss her on the mouth? she implored silently. Why didn't he leave her alone? Was his kiss heaven ... or was it hell? Whichever, it seemed to go on for a very long time.

'What was that for?' she asked stiffly as he stepped back behind her and released her hair.

'To send you off to sleep,' he replied, and strode away into his bedroom.

To Darcy's surprise she fell asleep quickly and in the morning, when they talked about her stage fright again, she did feel better. While Keir said that the Washington success had loaded the New York run with even greater expectations and reckoned that she could be reacting to the pressure of this, he did not harp on the subject. However, his attitude was so positive that during the day her belief in herself returned. She would not dry at this evening's performance, she told herself confidently.

Yet when they stood in the wings, waiting to make their entrances, tension gripped and her stomach started to churn. She felt *ill*.

As if sensing this, Keir put his arm around her. 'You'll be fine,' he declared.

'Will I?' Darcy asked, suddenly dreadfully doubtful.

'For sure.' On stage the line which cued in her appearance was spoken. 'Go get 'em, honey,' Keir said, and grinned.

Boosted by his certainty, his grin, and by that precious word 'honey', Darcy walked forward. Everything went perfectly until the final act, when something inside her brain seemed to jar. A wave of fear came over her. Oh, Lord, it was happening *again*.

Darcy was frantically wondering if she should try a silent song—which song? She could not think of a song. She did not know any songs—when Keir's eyes caught hers and his voice almost imperceptibly strengthened. He was adding emphasis to Marcus's words, forcing her to concentrate on her character and not on herself. She responded, and the fear evaporated.

To her enormous relief she suffered no more lapses and by the time the Washington run finished her sense of security was almost back in place. Almost, because the crucial test—the Broadway first night—still lay ahead. However, if she did mess up, although it would be traumatic for her, it would not cause the collapse of the production. Nor, as Keir had said, would it mean Armageddon.

As she took a last look through drawers, checking that she had not left anything before her case was fastened, ready for the flight to New York, her mood was pensive. While Keir cared about the play and would obviously not have wanted her stage fright to mar it, he had cared about *her* feelings too. The help he had given had been personal. And, whatever animosity he felt with regard to other aspects of their relationship, his help had been generous.

As a hands-on director he had myriad other matters which demanded his attention, and as the leading actor he had also had his input into his own role to think about. The demands on him were considerable, yet he had always been there to boost her spirits if they had shown sign of flagging and to encourage. She closed the locks on her suitcase. Keir was a caring individual with a big heart.

'Thank you for all your hospitality,' she said as they waited in the living-room for the cab which had been booked to take them to the airport, 'and thanks for helping me to conquer my stage fright. I'm very grateful.' She frowned at him as he belatedly repacked a too full holdall. 'I owe you an apology. I accused you of tyrannising my father, but I made a mistake. I know now that you'd never tyrannise.'

He stopped his repacking to look at her. Hard. 'That's a profound shift of opinion,' he remarked.

'Yes. And I suspect that his depression could've been due to his ego having taken some kind of a knock because——' she hesitated '—well, Rupert was extremely fond of himself.'

Keir forced a pair of training shoes in beside a couple of books. 'That shift's even profounder,' he said.

'Yes,' Darcy agreed again, and sighed. The acknowledgement that her father had had faults had stretched further and gone much deeper. She had begun mentally rummaging through their family past and the pictures she now saw with painful clarity made a stark contrast to the pictures which her mother had painted. 'When you heard that Rupert had died, why didn't you write?' she enquired.

'I did. I wrote to his wife—the third one—saying how sorry I was and asking her to pass on my condolences to you. Though,' he added, 'my letter would've been about three months late.'

'And by the time it arrived shortage of cash had meant that she'd had to leave the grand Knightsbridge house,' Darcy said pensively.

'So she never received it?'

'No.'

The doorbell rang. 'Time to go,' he said.

And my second stepmother not getting your letter is why I decided that you did not care about my father's death, she thought as she followed him out to the cab.

The house lights shone full on, every exit door had been opened wide, but still the audience refused to leave. As the standing ovation continued Keir took hold of Darcy's hand and once more led her to the front of the stage. The applause roared to a crescendo. There were deafening cheers and a chorus of piercing whistles. Darcy smiled out at the audience and turned to smile at Keir, who drew her close.

'You did it,' he whispered into her ear.

Her smile spread. Despite having felt increasingly conscious of the first night approaching and near to petrified for most of today, she had not dried. Keir's confidence in her had been catching and balm to her soul for, from taking her first step on to the stage, Darcy had known that she could cope, that the fright demon had been banished.

'No, *you* did it,' she argued.

He hugged her. '*We* did it,' he declared.

As they stepped back to allow the other members of the cast to take further bows Darcy noticed a woman clapping wildly in the first row of the stalls.

'That looks like Mrs Moblinski,' she said out of the side of her mouth.

'It is,' he agreed, and directed a special smile at his admirer, who fiercely nudged the women on either side of her as if to say, He remembers me! and clapped even louder.

Although the audience's reaction made a negative verdict from the Axe Man seem unlikely, as everyone assembled at the SoHo restaurant which Cal Warburg had reserved for a second first-night shindig, the mood was euphoric yet cautious. Nothing could be certain.

A meal was eaten, wine drunk and, after what seemed like forever, the morning's newspapers were brought in. Commandeering the first copy of the Axe Man's paper, Cal riffled through the pages and after a tense moment, when everyone in the restaurant fell silent and a pin could have been heard to drop, he gave a whoop of joy.

'"Deeply compassionate and darkly humorous play,"' the producer read, plucking out random sentences. '"The power of Keir Robards' acting is impossible to ignore. He's sensational and so is Darcy Weston, the daughter of the late, great Sir Rupert. It'll be a long time before we see such fine performances again. So moved by the concluding passages of the play, I had tears in my eyes.'''

'The Axe Man cries?' squealed Thea, giving a little shimmy of amazement, and everyone laughed.

'''Best work Keir Robards has done as a director,''' Cal continued. '''I recommend everyone to go and see it.''' There was another whoop of joy. 'We have a hit on our hands, kids!'

Although the celebrating which followed seemed destined to continue until daybreak, a short while later Darcy started to say her goodbyes. Sapped of energy, the prospect of all-night hilarity held little appeal and she longed to be quiet.

'I'm exhausted,' she explained to Cal, and the producer fondly patted her hand and assured her that he understood.

'I'll come with you,' Keir said when she told him she was leaving.

'There's no need,' she demurred. 'I'll be perfectly safe in a cab and it's not far.'

For the run of the play they were staying in apartments in a modern tower block close to Central Park. She and Keir were next door to each other on the fifth floor, while the other actors were dotted around elsewhere. Designed to accommodate holidaymakers, the one-bedroom apartments had spacious living-rooms, well-equipped kitchen areas and were attractively furnished.

'But I'm worn out too,' he told her. 'I read somewhere that the stress experienced by leading actors on an important opening night is the equivalent to driving a car into a brick wall at thirty miles an hour.' Wearily he raked back his hair. 'Right now, it feels like it.'

Farewells were said and, to a chorus of cheers, they departed.

'It seems as if Cal will be giving the trust a large donation,' Darcy commented as the lift carried them up to their apartments.

'It does,' Keir agreed, smiling. 'It also looks as though you'll be inundated with offers of top-line roles. Are you still thinking you'll refuse them?'

'Definitely.'

He regarded her in silence for a moment. 'Come and have a drink with me before you go to bed,' he said.

Darcy hesitated. The habit of a late-night chat had ended with their transfer to New York a few days ago, but did she want to resurrect it? Wouldn't it be wiser, now that they were living apart, to separate herself from him as much as possible? A chill settled around her heart. After all, once the play ended they would be going their different ways.

'There's something I need to explain,' Keir continued when she looked doubtful.

She shrugged. 'OK.'

She had only agreed because she wanted to hear what it was he had to say, she told herself as she accompanied him into his apartment, and because no matter how exhausted she felt it seemed unlikely that she would sleep.

In the short, work-intensive time they had been in New York there had been no opportunity for shopping, but a basket of basic groceries had been supplied to each apartment and so Keir was able to make two mugs of instant coffee.

'I wasn't going to tell you this,' he said gravely as they carried their drinks into the living area, 'but circumstances change.' He levered himself down into the large grey and gold armchair opposite hers. 'Rupert suffered from stage fright too.'

Darcy stared at him in astonishment. Her father's self-assurance had always seemed so buoyant and invincible—yet . . . yet suddenly she was aware of pieces of a jigsaw slotting into place. And of questions being answered.

'Which is why he became depressed?' she said.

Keir nodded. 'Apparently he'd had one or two uncomfortable moments in the previous play he'd been in, but had gotten over them. When we first started rehearsing Rupert gave all the appearance of being relaxed and yet, in a very short time, he became uptight. I don't know if you remember, but halfway through the rehearsals he took part in a benefit evening for a fellow actor who had cancer.'

'I do remember,' she told him.

'Well, his contribution was a solo reading, and the next day when I asked him how it'd gone he became damn near hysterical. He said he'd lost the lines and spoken gobbledegook. Maybe he had, but there were no adverse comments and no one seemed to have noticed.

'However, the experience scared him half to death and weighed on his mind. As our rehearsals continued he'd get me alone and start talking about other actors who had suffered stage fright, walked off the stage at the interval and never walked back again. Ever.

'He gradually convinced himself he was fated to break down in the play, it'd be headlines in all the newspapers, and that his career would go into a tailspin. I told him he was wrong and said that if the worst should happen he'd soon make it back to the top again, like others had done, but he wasn't having any.'

'And that's why he withdrew?'

'Yes. I did my damnedest to persuade him he could overcome the problem——'

'Like you did with me,' Darcy cut in.

Keir nodded. 'But you have a more realistic view of being an actor, so you were more open to persuasion.'

'Did you tell my father that acting wasn't the be-all and end-all?' she enquired.

'Several times,' he said, and gave a wry smile, 'but as far as he was concerned I was speaking heresy. He took his profession, and himself, ultra-seriously.

'Rupert begged me not to tell anyone the real reason for his withdrawal, hence the "artistic differences" fudge,' Keir continued. 'He was terrified of rumours starting about him being unreliable and then people might hesitate to cast him.'

'So he thought he'd get over his stage fright?'

'He vowed that he would, given time, though to me he seemed doubtful. And his depression would indicate that he quickly abandoned all hope.'

Darcy sighed. 'I didn't know any of this.'

'No, as far as I'm aware Rupert only spoke of his fears to me. However, when I rang to ask how he was feeling I got very short shrift, so it seemed he'd regretted taking me into his confidence.

'But the reason Rupert didn't tell you was because he would've hated to have seemed less than perfect in your eyes. And that's why *I* kept quiet. You once said your mother considered him to be a god and for a long time it seemed like you did too,' Keir explained. 'I was reluctant to spoil the image.'

'Thanks, but I don't have any illusions now,' she told him, a little sadly.

'I gathered that. Rupert once told me you were the only person in the world whom he'd ever truly cared about——'

'No,' Darcy interrupted. 'The only person Rupert ever truly cared about was himself.'

Keir gave her a thoughtful look. 'You think so?'

'I do. For example, the reason he wanted me to appear on Broadway was that it'd reflect well on him.' Her smile was dry. 'And if he could read tonight's reviews, although he'd be proud of me, the part which would please him most, which he'd centre on, would be the bit about the "late, *great* Sir Rupert". That's what would matter. His praise and glory, not mine.'

'I'm afraid so,' he acknowledged.

'When I was little Rupert was very affectionate and made a great fuss of me,' she went on. 'He liked us to be photographed together and he did again when I grew up. But there was a period in between when he refused all photographs, when he stopped coming to see me.'

Darcy swallowed. Her throat had stiffened. But after keeping silent about her father for so long, after denying the truth about him, even to herself, she *needed* to talk, no matter how painful the revelations.

'I was between ten and twelve at the time, and I was plump.'

'You had puppy fat?' Keir enquired.

'Yes, and braces on my teeth. I didn't look too good, though I didn't look too bad either—just a normal kid going through the stages of growing up. Yet Rupert——' her throat had constricted again and it took a moment to get the words out ' —lost all interest in me. He didn't remember my birthdays, send presents or even a card, and it hurt tremendously.

'I kept asking my mother why he didn't visit any more, and she maintained that he wanted to but he was too busy.' Darcy pressed her lips together. 'But I knew that I'd ceased to appeal,' she said in a choked voice. 'I'd seen it in his eyes.'

Keir set down his coffee-mug on the side-table. 'Come here,' he said softly.

'Sorry?'

He held out his arms. 'Come here.'

Rising, Darcy crossed to put her coffee down beside his and sit on his knee. For a moment she sat stiffly, but when he put his arm around her she rested against him.

'I never said anything,' she carried on, 'I just went along with my mother's excuses and tried to blank his distaste out of my mind, but——' her voice shook '—how could he have been so cruel?'

'Oh, honey,' Keir said gently, and she laid her head on his shoulder and started to cry.

It was like the floodgates opening. All the years of hurt and pain were washed out, together with the pretence and denial which her mother had forced on her. The tears fell for a long time and as they fell Keir held her close. But eventually her sobbing ceased, Darcy blew her nose and recovered.

'When my puppy fat and the braces disappeared Rupert turned up again,' she continued, determined to tell him the full story. 'He bought me a beautiful velvet cape with a fur-lined hood which I didn't see as a guilt-offering until much later.'

She gave a dry smile. 'Though I don't suppose he saw it that way or thought he'd been particularly cruel, because he never thought much about other people, about their feelings and how he hurt them. He was too damn self-centred.'

'And you were brainwashed into adoring him by your mother,' Keir said sombrely.

'Yes; she was unreliable where Rupert was concerned. They call it love,' Darcy remarked whimsically. 'But when you've been told from birth that your father's marvellous—and he could be *so* charming and such fun—it's a difficult idea to shake off. And I don't think I ever will—a part of me still loves him, no matter how he behaved.

'I also think that my stage fright could've had something to do with me wanting to do well for him,' she went on. Her shoulders moved in an aimless shrug. 'It's crazy, but——'

'Rupert was the most captivating guy.'

'And a bastard.'

Keir nodded. 'Unfortunately—yes.'

'I was also brainwashed into becoming an actress,' Darcy continued.

'Do you think Rupert fancied starting a theatrical dynasty?'

'Probably. It's the kind of thing which would've appealed to his ego, and he was always encouraging when I was in school plays and later when I attended stage school.' She sighed. 'But my becoming an actress also satisfied my mother's needs.'

'What needs?' Keir asked.

'With hindsight I think she felt that if I went into the same profession as my father it'd ensure that I had continuing contact with him, and therefore so would she. Whereas if I'd done something else he could've drifted out of my life—and hers.'

Darcy frowned. 'Although I've enjoyed acting I don't think I'm basically suited to the lifestyle. I'm not the kind who touts for work and I hate giving interviews and being noticed. And even if I have won an award I always feel like I'm a bit of a fraud.'

'So you're serious about giving it up?' he enquired.

'Yes. Now that my parents are no longer around to put pressure on me I'm far less keen. I don't know that I'll stop acting in total, but I intend to take time off to think about which way I want the rest of my life to go and consider other options.'

She looked at the side-table and their mugs of coffee, which she knew must now be cold. 'Would you like a fresh coffee?' she asked, rising to her feet.

'Please.'

Darcy collected the mugs. Making fresh drinks had been an excuse to get off his knee. She had been enjoying it too much and starting to feel as if she belonged there, and yet, no matter how kind and sympathetic Keir might be, their relationship was destined to finish when the run of the play ended.

'One thing I don't understand,' he said as she walked to the kitchen area, 'is why you went out with Gideon McCall. The guy may be good-looking in a fleshy kind of way, but frankly he's a smoothie so——'

'I went out with him on the rebound—from you. You wouldn't even kiss me but he did, within minutes of our being introduced, and at that particular time I needed to be kissed. Or thought I did.' She shot him a look. 'It'd been degrading when you refused to sleep with me, so when Gideon showed an interest——'

'I refused to sleep with you?' Keir enquired.

Darcy plugged in the kettle and switched it on. 'You did—when I came to see you at the Brierly.'

'That's what you wanted?' he demanded. 'That's what you were asking?'

'What else?'

Keir swore. 'God Almighty,' he said in an anguished voice, 'I sure bungled that one. I thought you were asking me to marry you.'

CHAPTER NINE

DARCY gave a startled laugh. 'Marry you? But we'd only known each other a month and I was barely eighteen,' she protested, thinking that she would never have had the courage nor the confidence to propose to him, even if it had occurred to her. 'And we hadn't even kissed.'

'Sure, but Suzanne said——'

'Said what?' she asked when Keir broke off to frown. She concentrated on spooning coffee granules into the mugs. 'I realise you're still keen on Suzanne, but you might as well know that I never——'

'I'm not keen.'

She looked up. 'But when you talked about her being married you seemed . . . bothered.'

'I was. I am.' He frowned again. 'When you've made the coffee I'll explain.'

Fascinated to hear what he had to say, she quickly prepared the drinks, then, 'I'm ready,' Darcy declared, handing him his mug and sitting down again in her armchair.

'I need to start way back,' he began slowly. 'Before I came over to London seven years ago I'd been living with a girl. We were both keen on our careers—she worked in advertising—and neither of us wanted to get married, but our relationship was good.

'However, after about eighteen months she was offered a job in California and so we decided to call it a day. Because it'd always been accepted that we weren't together for the long term, it was an amicable parting.'

Keir tasted his coffee. 'I already knew Suzanne through mutual friends, and when she heard I was on my own again she rang to say she needed a partner for an office dinner and would I accompany her. I agreed, and after that we started going out from time to time.'

'You asked her?'

He shook his head. 'She always asked me. It's called feminism,' he said drily. 'But pretty soon she started dropping hints about the two of us getting together seriously.'

'You weren't interested?' Darcy asked when he grimaced.

'No. Suzanne was pleasant enough company, but not my type.'

She looked at him over the rim of her mug. 'Meaning?'

'Too slick, too hard. Though in any case,' he continued, 'having just ended one relationship, I was in no hurry to become involved in another. However, Suzanne kept on hinting and increasing the pressure—so much so that it was a relief to get away to London. I hoped that in my absence it'd dawn on her that a romance with me was a non-starter, but I'd no sooner unpacked my case at the Brierly than she was on the phone.'

He groaned. 'Suzanne rang me every single day. She insisted on knowing what I'd been doing, so I explained how we were looking around the city together.'

'You thought that telling her about being with another girl might show you felt no commitment to her?'

'There could've been something of that in it, though we were having such a great time that I was just happy to talk. However, the next thing I knew, the bloody woman arrived at the hotel and asked me to marry her!'

'Boy, oh, boy,' Darcy said.

'Quite. Suzanne knew our friendship was tepid at best, and yet she put me in the embarrassing position of having to say no. Not that she took my refusal as final and flew home. No siree,' Keir said pungently. 'She declared that she'd stay for a while and give me time to think it over.

'Later that day she turned up, uninvited, at the theatre where we were shortly due to start rehearsals, and I saw her talking to the stage manager. Afterwards she told me that he'd told her how you were keen to marry me. That marriage was what you expected. I said I didn't believe her and she was making it up, but a couple of evenings later——'

'I appeared in your bedroom and started to propose, as you thought.'

'Yes, and I panicked.'

Darcy's brow creased. 'But I only came to the Brierly because of Suzanne. We'd spoken at my father's party and she'd claimed that you'd found it "a giggle" to be taken around London by a teenager.'

He shook his head. 'I never said that. I enjoyed us being together.'

'I thought you did, though Suzanne made me unsure. It's obvious now that she was warning me off,' Darcy went on, 'but she made me feel like a child, which in turn made me determined to show you that I was grown-up.'

'And, in your *femme fatale* dress, you well and truly did,' he remarked, with a dry inflexion. He paused. 'But, at that particular time, I was too involved in my career to consider marriage—to anyone. I can see that my rejection must've come over as harsh——'

'And arrogant,' she said.

'I guess. But I was so damn shocked. First Suzanne had proposed and next minute you appeared to be wanting to march me up the aisle. I felt beleaguered, attacked from all sides. I was attempting to calm down and explain that marriage could have no place on my agenda right then, when you rushed out.

'I didn't know what to do. I decided to let the situation lie for a while, became involved in the rehearsals and—what do you know?—someone told me you were going out with Gideon McCall.' His brow furrowed. 'I was so jealous.'

'Jealous?' she enquired.

'When I read the account of your lovemaking I wanted to strangle the guy.'

'Why? I realise I attracted you a bit, but——'

'A bit?' Keir protested. 'I'd fallen in love with you.'

Darcy gave him a dubious look. 'You had?'

'Yes, though I didn't realise it then, nor for years after.'

'When did you realise?' she asked.

'When we made love; that made it clear beyond all doubt. But when I'd spoken about you on the phone to Suzanne she'd recognised the depth of my feelings, even if I hadn't,' Keir remarked cryptically, 'which is why she flew over. She believed I was heading towards something serious, so she proposed in an attempt to head you off and get in first.'

'Suzanne told you this?' Darcy enquired.

He nodded. 'Just before she departed for the States, in one heck of a fury, after she'd finally accepted that she and I had no future.'

He took another drink of coffee. 'Although *I* wouldn't accept that I loved you, you were the reason why I steered clear of London for all those years afterwards. I felt uneasy about the prospect of running into you again— though,' he added, with a wry smile, 'that didn't stop me from thinking about you, or buying the English newspapers in the hope of reading your name, or keeping an ear open for any gossip.'

'But you came over to see me in the award-winning play,' she protested.

'Yes. Eventually I lost patience with myself. I decided that if I saw you again it'd be one big anticlimax and I'd realise that whatever my feelings had been they were long gone.' Keir drank the last of his coffee and set down his cup. 'I was wrong. You were still special and I continued to feel...something. So when Bill Shapiro fell by the wayside——'

'You agreed to direct the play because of me?' Darcy said in astonishment.

'I did.'

'But I thought you had to be persuaded?'

'I was playing hard to get, though I'd have done it on whatever terms Cal Warburg had offered, if necessary. Maurice had said you didn't have a boyfriend,' he continued, 'so I decided to take a chance and see how things developed between us. But when we met you were so hostile and that first kiss...' He rolled his eyes. 'There was no reaction.'

'I was surprised,' Darcy protested, and she lowered her eyes. 'The next one was better.'

'Much,' Keir said, with a grin. 'It was all I could do to keep my eyes from dancing. But when you continued to be hostile, and yet were kissing me as though you meant it in our rehearsals, I didn't know what to think.'

'You must've realised my hostility was tied in with my father,' she said.

'I did, and for a while I wondered if he'd told you I was to blame for his loss of confidence, but it turned out that he'd said nothing. In the midst of all this I had yet to decide exactly what I felt about you. You were driving me crazy with lust, but what about love? Then we slept together and I knew it was the real thing.'

Keir sucked in his lower lip. 'When I realised you were a virgin it seemed as if you'd been saving yourself for me and I felt so *grateful*, but then——'

Her stomach hollowed. 'Then I told you I'd been using you,' she said.

He gave a twisted smile. 'It was the all-time humbler.'

'And killed your love for me stone-dead,' she said, her tone lifeless too.

'No,' Keir said.

'It—it didn't?' Darcy asked tremulously.

'I love you, now and forever. I said once that I cared intensely and it's you I care intensely about.'

'But when we kiss on stage now you don't...react,' she protested.

'No, and have you any idea what hard work it is keeping my feelings under control—both on stage and here now?' Keir demanded, sounding suddenly angry.

'You don't have to keep your feelings under control now,' Darcy said, going to sit on his knee again. Her exhaustion had gone, and although it was the early hours of the morning she felt zingingly alive. She wound an arm around his neck. 'You see, I love you too.'

'Love me or lust after me?' he enquired, as if wary of being cajoled. 'I know you're a hot lady, but——'

'I love you, with all my heart,' she assured him, 'and have done since we first met. That's why I slept with you, why I waited for so long.' Abruptly, she frowned. 'If you were never keen on Suzanne, why do you feel bad about her marriage?'

'Because, just as you became involved with Gideon McCall on the rebound, she came back to the States and within months married some guy,' he explained. 'Unfortunately the marriage has never been happy and I feel partway responsible.'

'But chances are that Suzanne pressurised the man into marrying her,' she protested.

'I believe she did,' he acknowledged.

'So the state of her marriage is her fault, not yours.' He nodded. 'You're right.'

'You needn't have felt jealous about Gideon,' Darcy went on, 'because when he kissed me I used to close my eyes and pretend it was you. And when I opened them again—yuck!—it was such a disappointment.'

'I should hope so; I'm far better looking,' Keir said, with a grin.

She poked him in the chest. 'In your opinion.'

'And in yours. Right?'

She laughed. 'Right.'

'Do you think you could stop talking about Suzanne and Gideon, and give us a chance to talk about us?' he demanded.

She nestled against him. The concept of 'us' made her feel warm and cherished. 'What about us?' she enquired a little breathlessly.

'About the fact that if I'd agreed to sleep with you at the Brierly and we'd started an affair you would've expected me to marry you.'

Darcy sighed. 'I suppose so, though I would've been far too young.'

'But now you're seven years older, so...?' Keir lifted expectant brows.

Her heart sang. 'Is this a proposal?' she asked.

'Darcy, we've been apart far too long and I need you beside me—as my wife,' he told her seriously. 'You said you were going to consider other options than full-time acting and marrying me is one, so why don't you sleep on the idea? In my bed.'

She smiled at him, her eyes radiant. 'I don't need to; the answer's yes. But I will sleep in your bed.' Standing up, Darcy held out a hand. 'Hurry,' she said.

Her undisguised eagerness made Keir's lips twitch with laughter. But he did hurry, whisking her into the bedroom and swiftly undressing her, though when they were both naked and lying in bed his haste slowed.

Lifting her chin to tilt her head, he looked deep into her eyes, told her again of his love for her, and started raining exquisitely lingering kisses upon her. For a while they were content just to kiss, to explore each other's mouths, to enjoy the taste of each other. Then hands began to move, to fondle and touch.

'I want to feel you all over, every inch of you,' Keir murmured as his hand stroked over the high curve of her breast and down her body to rest on the silkiness of her thigh.

'Ditto,' she said, running her fingers over his chest, touching first one flat brown nipple and then the other.

'I like that,' he told her. 'Some men don't, but I do.'

So she lowered her head and kissed and licked his nipples, until a shudder went through him and he steered her back on to the bed.

'My turn,' he said huskily.

As his tongue lapped over the tightening peaks of her breasts, an aching intensity started to gnaw inside her. And as she felt his body grow greedy and acquisitive Darcy strained closer. She loved this beautiful man with all her heart and soul, and with all her body. She could feel her love for him in her fingers, in her toes, could feel it pounding in her heart.

His tanned hand slid between the milky whiteness of her thighs and the world began to spin. He straddled her, and as she felt the thrust of his entering her Darcy cried out his name. Their breathing rasped loud in the silent, night-dark room. Sweat glistened on heated skin. Darcy reached heights of desire she had not known were possible. In one final, glorious, flooding moment he made her his and again she touched the moon...and the sun...and the stars.

'I'm like my mother,' Darcy murmured a long time later, when they had made love again and pale streaks of dawn were beginning to lighten the New York sky. 'I'm a one-man woman.'

Keir's lips curved. 'So you'll be treating me like a god?'

'You mean put you on a pedestal and worship you from afar?' she teased.

'No, thanks! I'll settle for being treated like a mortal man.' He drew her closer. 'A man who needs to be made love to.'

'A third time?' she protested, her eyes shining.

'We have seven years to catch up on.'

'Which is a lot of catching up to do, so——' she heaved a sigh of mock despair '—I guess we'd better make a start.'

Keir kissed her. 'Right now, honey,' he agreed. 'Right now.'

Coming Next Month

HARLEQUIN PRESENTS®

THE BEST HAS JUST GOTTEN BETTER

#1833 THE FATHER OF HER CHILD Emma Darcy
Lauren didn't want to fall in love again—but when she saw Michael all her good resolutions went out the window. And when she learned he was out to break her heart she vowed never to see him again. But it was too late....

#1834 WILD HUNGER Charlotte Lamb
Book Four: *SINS*
Why was Gerard, famous foreign correspondent, following Keira? She could hardly believe he was interested in the story of a supermodel fighting a constant battle with food. No, he wanted something more....

#1835 THE TROPHY HUSBAND Lynne Graham
(9 to 5)
When Sara caught her fiancé being unfaithful, her boss, Alex, helped pick up the pieces of her life. But Sara wondered what price she would have to pay for his unprecedented kindness.

#1836 THE STRENGTH OF DESIRE Alison Fraser
(This Time, Forever)
The death of Hope's husband brought his brother, Guy, back into her life, and left her with two legacies. Both meant that neither Hope nor Guy would be able to forget their erstwhile short-lived affair.

#1837 FRANCESCA Sally Wentworth
(Ties of Passion, 2)
Francesca was used to having the best of everything—and that included men. The uncouth Sam was a far cry from her usual boyfriends, but he was the only man who had ever loved her for what she was rather than what she had.

#1838 TERMS OF POSSESSION Elizabeth Power
Nadine needed money—and Cameron needed a child. His offer was extraordinary—he would possess her body and soul and the resulting baby would be his. But the arrangements were becoming complicated...

MILLION DOLLAR SWEEPSTAKES
AND
EXTRA BONUS PRIZE DRAWING

No purchase necessary. To enter the sweepstakes, follow the directions published and complete and mail your Official Entry Form. If your Official Entry Form is missing, or you wish to obtain an additional one (limit: one Official Entry Form per request, one request per outer mailing envelope) send a separate, stamped, self-addressed #10 envelope (4 1/8" X 9 1/2") via first class mail to: Million Dollar Sweepstakes and Extra Bonus Prize Drawing Entry Form, P.O. Box 1867, Buffalo, NY 14269-1867. Request must be received no later than January 15, 1998. For eligibility into the sweepstakes, entries must be received no later than March 31,1998. No liability is assumed for printing errors, lost, late, non-delivered or misdirected entries. Odds of winning are determined by the number of eligible entries distributed and received.

Sweepstakes open to residents of the U.S. (except Puerto Rico), Canada and Europe who are 18 years of age or older. All applicable laws and regulations apply. Sweepstakes offer void wherever prohibited by law. Values of all prizes are in U.S. currency. This sweepstakes is presented by Torstar Corp., its subsidiaries and affiliates, in conjunction with book, merchandise and/or product offerings. For a copy of the Official Rules governing this sweepstakes, send a self-addressed, stamped envelope (WA residents need not affix return postage) to: MILLION DOLLAR SWEEP-STAKES AND EXTRA BONUS PRIZE DRAWING Rules, P.O. Box 4470, Blair, NE 68009-4470, USA.

FAST CASH 4032 DRAW RULES
NO PURCHASE OR OBLIGATION NECESSARY

Fifty prizes of $50 each will be awarded in random drawings to be conducted no later than 11/28/96 from amongst all eligible responses to this prize offer received as of 10/15/96. To enter, follow directions, affix 1st-class postage and mail OR write Fast Cash 4032 on a 3" x 5" card along with your name and address and mail that card to: Harlequin's Fast Cash 4032 Draw, P.O. Box 1395, Buffalo, NY 14240-1395 OR P.O. Box 618, Fort Erie, Ontario L2A 5X3. (Limit: one entry per outer envelope; all entries must be sent via 1st-class mail.) Limit: one prize per household. Odds of winning are determined by the number of eligible responses received. Offer is open only to residents of the U.S. (except Puerto Rico) and Canada and is void wherever prohibited by law. All applicable laws and regulations apply. Any litigation within the province of Quebec respecting the conduct and awarding of a prize in this sweepstakes may be submitted to the Régie des alcools, des courses et des jeux. In order for a Canadian resident to win a prize, that person will be required to correctly answer a time-limited arithmetical skill-testing question to be administered by mail. Names of winners available after 12/28/96 by sending a self-addressed, stamped envelope to: Fast Cash 4032 Draw Winners, P.O. Box 4200, Blair, NE 68009-4200.

SWP-H8ZD

HARLEQUIN PRESENTS®

Ties of Passion
by Sally Wentworth

The story of the Brodey family. Money, looks, style—the
Brodeys have everything...except love.

Read part one of this exciting three-part series

#1832 CHRIS

Chris Brodey could offer Tiffany anything she wanted,
but she soon discovered that he wasn't a man prepared to
give something for nothing....

Watch for books two and three in
September and October!

Available in August wherever Harlequin books are sold.

Look us up on-line at: http://www.romance.net

Free Gift Offer

As Seen on TV!

With a Free Gift proof-of-purchase
from any Harlequin® book, you can receive
a beautiful cubic zirconia pendant.

This stunning marquise-shaped stone is a genuine cubic
zirconia—accented by an 18" gold tone necklace.
(Approximate retail value $19.95)

Send for yours today...
compliments of ◆HARLEQUIN®

To receive your free gift, a cubic zirconia pendant, send us one original proof-of-
purchase, photocopies not accepted, from the back of any Harlequin Romance®,
Harlequin Presents®, Harlequin Temptation®, Harlequin Superromance®, Harlequin
Intrigue®, Harlequin American Romance®, or Harlequin Historicals® title available in
August, September or October at your favorite retail outlet, together with the Free Gift
Certificate, plus a check or money order for $1.65 U.S./$2.15 CAN. (do not send cash) to
cover postage and handling, payable to Harlequin Free Gift Offer. We will send you the
specified gift. Allow 6 to 8 weeks for delivery. Offer good until October 31, 1996 or while
quantities last. Offer valid in the U.S. and Canada only.

Free Gift Certificate

Name: _____

Address: _____

City: _____ State/Province: _____ Zip/Postal Code: _____

Mail this certificate, one proof-of-purchase and a check or money order for postage
and handling to: HARLEQUIN FREE GIFT OFFER 1996. In the U.S.: 3010 Walden
Avenue, P.O. Box 9071, Buffalo NY 14269-9057. In Canada: P.O. Box 604, Fort Erie,
Ontario L2Z 5X3.

FREE GIFT OFFER   084-KMF

ONE PROOF-OF-PURCHASE
To collect your fabulous FREE GIFT, a cubic zirconia pendant, you must include this
original proof-of-purchase for each gift with the properly completed Free Gift Certificate.

084-KMF

HARLEQUIN PRESENTS®

Love can conquer the deadliest of !

Indulge in Charlotte Lamb's exciting seven-part series

Watch for:

The Sin of Gluttony
in

#1834 WILD HUNGER

Why was Gerard, the famous journalist, following Keira?
She could hardly believe he was interested in the story of
a supermodel fighting a battle with food....

Available in September wherever
Harlequin books are sold.

Look us up on-line at: http://www.romance.net

SINS4

You're About to Become a *Privileged Woman*

Reap the rewards of fabulous free gifts and benefits with proofs-of-purchase from Harlequin and Silhouette books

Pages & Privileges™

It's our way of thanking you for buying our books at your favorite retail stores.

✂ PROOF OF PURCHASE
HP-PP161
Offer expires October 31, 1996

Pages & Privileges™

**Harlequin and Silhouette—
the most privileged readers in the world!**

For more information about Harlequin and Silhouette's PAGES & PRIVILEGES program call the Pages & Privileges Benefits Desk: 1-503-794-2499

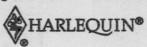
HARLEQUIN®

HP-PP161